"Are you still frightened and confused?"

He tilted his elegant head, taking in her protective posture.

"Yes," she said, her voice cracking.

A hint of that knowing smile slid across his lips. "Would you like me to go, then?"

For several pounding heartbeats they stood in absolute silence—each taking the measure of the other.

"Well?"

"No," she whispered, barely keeping the panic at bay. Panic…and something else. *Excitement.*

With a blaze of heat, she realized she wanted to touch him. Wanted to explore his magnificent body with her own hands. Wanted to learn what a man from another planet felt like. What moved him. What made him cry out. What it felt like to be with him, intimately. This time it wasn't some weird effect of his touching her.

And suddenly, she could think of nothing but the searing, sensual kiss they'd shared.

Dear Reader,

Wow. I'll bet you think I've finally lost it! First a hero who's a ghost, then one with a transmigrated body and now…dare I say it? Yep. An alien hero. The kind from outer space. Yikes! What is with that Nina Bruhns lately?

I guess my books have always been about outsiders, loners. Heroes and heroines who don't fit in, but who long for love and community, as we all do. What is more of an outsider than a guy from another galaxy? And what a guy! Carch Sunstryker is out of this world. A tall, golden prince who knows just what every woman wants. Did I mention he's a shapeshifter?

Anyway, I hope you are enjoying the lighter, snappier page-turners I've been writing lately. I'm having loads of fun with these new stories. And they don't stop with this one. Be sure to pick up my June release from Silhouette Romantic Suspense. Think sex and murder on the beach. Trust me, you won't want to miss the adventure!

Until then, please check out my newly redesigned Web site, www.NinaBruhns.com, and drop me a line!

Good reading!

Nina

THE REBEL
PRINCE

Nina Bruhns

Romantic
SUSPENSE

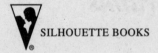 SILHOUETTE BOOKS

ISBN-13: 978-0-373-27574-8
ISBN-10:   0-373-27574-9

THE REBEL PRINCE

Visit Silhouette Books at www.eHarlequin.com

Printed in U.S.A.

Books by Nina Bruhns

Silhouette Romantic Suspense

Catch Me If You Can #990
Warrior's Bride #1080
Sweet Revenge #1163
Sins of the Father #1209
Sweet Suspicion #1277
Ghost of a Chance #1319
Blue Jeans and a Badge #1361
Hard Case Cowboy #1385
Enemy Husband #1402
Royal Betrayal #1424
The Forbidden Enchantment #1454
Top-Secret Bride #1480
The Rebel Prince #1504

Silhouette Nocturne

Night Mischief #25

NINA BRUHNS

credits her Gypsy great-grandfather for her great love of adventure. Nina has lived and traveled all over the world, including a six-year stint in Sweden and has been on scientific expeditions to such diverse places as California, Spain, Egypt and the Sudan. She has two graduate degrees in archaeology (with a specialty in Egyptology), she speaks four languages and she writes a mean hieroglyphic!

But Nina's first love has always been writing. For her, writing for Silhouette Books is the ultimate adventure. Drawing on her many experiences gives her stories a colorful dimension and allows her to create settings and characters out of the ordinary. She has won numerous awards for her previous titles including a prestigious National Readers Choice Award, two Daphne DuMaurier awards of Excellence for Overall Best Romantic Suspense of the year, five Dorothy Parker awards and two Golden Hearts awards, among many others.

A native of Canada, Nina grew up in California and currently resides in Charleston, South Carolina, with her husband and three children. She loves to hear from her readers and can be reached at P.O. Box 2216 or Summerville, SC 29484-2216 or by e-mail via her Web site, www.NinaBruhns.com, or via the Harlequin Web site, www.eHarlequin.com.

For all the wonderful Silhouette Intimate Moments and Silhouette Romantic Suspense authors with whom I have played and worked. You ladies are the classiest, most talented group of people I've ever had the privilege of knowing. Go SRS!

Love, Nina

Chapter 1

Present day, Charleston, South Carolina, Earth

Something was wrong. She could feel it.

And feelings were not something Serenity June Woodson usually had, or paid attention to.

Okay, that wasn't strictly true. She had plenty of feelings, Seri told herself as she circled her rental car around the crowded downtown block again, searching in vain for a parking spot. Just not *those* kinds of feelings. You know, those woo-woo, New Age, "Irish Gift" kinds of feelings. The kind with which her Aunt Tildy made a living at the Second Sun Crystal and Tarot Salon, bless her eccentric heart.

Come on, come on. After a third circuit of the area around Queen Street, Seri jetted out an impatient breath, gave up and headed for a nearby parking garage. She had to hurry!

Aunt Tildy had phoned her last night all upset because

someone had stolen her favorite necklace. *Favorite* being an understatement. A *huge* understatement. In truth, the unusual star-shaped gold-and-gemstone necklace hadn't left its place of honor around Aunt Tildy's neck for over forty years. Forty-*two* to be exact. Ever since the fateful night she claimed it was placed there by—

Yeah. Well. Never mind who it had been placed there by. Aunt Tildy was prone to bouts of imagination. *Vivid* imagination. After all, look how she made her living—reading tarot cards and telling peoples' fortunes. Yes, okay, if Seri were completely objective—and Seri was always objective—she'd have to admit her loveable aunt had an unusual…knack…for predicting the future. Sort of. Still, you couldn't take a lot of things Aunt Tildy said seriously.

Which was why Seri hadn't taken it very seriously last night when her aunt had told her *not* to come to Charleston, that she was going to report the robbery to the police, and besides, she had a new friend who was going to help her check the pawn shops and antique dealers to try and find the priceless necklace.

Hello? A new friend?

Seri quickly locked the car and hurried toward Queen Street. *What* new friend? Her aunt wouldn't even tell her his name. That's right. *His* name. Good lord, it had been forty-two years since Aunt Tildy had gotten involved with a man, and she was still pining for the jerk. Somehow that long-ago con man had convinced her he was a prince from another planet—of all the ridiculous nonsense—and when he'd left her behind, a tearful and heartbroken twenty-year-old girl, he'd actually had the gall to tell her that one day he'd return to Earth to fetch her.

Talk about your vivid imagination.

And your naive gullibility.

Thank goodness it wasn't the same guy who'd returned.

Still, Seri wondered who this new con man was that her too-trusting aunt had gotten herself involved with. Not that she wasn't always enmeshed in one craziness or another, but this time Seri was genuinely worried. On the phone her aunt had sounded…different. She'd been frantic over the loss of her necklace, and yet, she'd also seemed…excited. Because of this mysterious male *friend?*

Naturally, Seri had jumped on the first flight from Phoenix to Charleston that morning. Despite the denials, her aunt needed her. This necklace meant more to Aunt Tildy than anything else in the world. And she had always been there for Seri, through thick and thin. Especially through thin. The least she could do was return the favor. Ever since speaking with her yesterday, Seri just couldn't shake the feeling—an instinct—that something momentous was about to happen, and that she had to get to the Second Sun Crystal and Tarot Salon to stop it. *Quickly.*

Ducking into the shady, arched French-Quarter-style passageway between the Thin Man Art Deco Gallery and the Old World Rare and Antique Bookstore, she almost stumbled over a homeless person sitting against the cool brick wall, his ragged belongings in a black plastic bag next to him.

"Oh! Sorry, didn't see you." She skirted around his Air Jordans as he mumbled an apology for blocking the passage, then raced precariously over the uneven cobblestones past Madam Clarissa's Palmistry Shoppe. Rushing along the path of lush foliage, she finally reached the entrance to her aunt's tarot salon, which was situated at the end of the quaint, flower-filled courtyard. And was brought up short.

It was closed.

A hastily scribbled note was taped to the pretty, multicolored stained-glass door: Gone to the hoosegow to report a theft. Will return when I return. May the stars guide you!

Anxiously, Seri glanced in through the sidelights. Everything looked just as it should inside. Peaceful. Orderly. No sign of anything amiss. She looked up and checked the second-story windows of the apartment where Aunt Tildy lived over the salon. One of the casements was open to the cool courtyard air, a curtain fluttering out from it in the slight breeze, along with a drift of patchouli.

No noises. No screams. No con men.

Aunt Tildy was fine.

All the anxiety whooshed out of Seri on a relieved exhale and an embarrassed laugh. So much for instincts.

This was why Aunt Tildy was the psychic, and not her.

She really should just stick to her science experiments. Logic and reasoning, those were the only things a person could truly depend on. Seri had no business acting on impulse or fuzzy, nebulous "feelings." She knew better.

With a relieved smile, she shook her head over the imagined urgency she'd felt earlier. Utter nonsense.

But she wasn't sorry she'd come. Her summer vacation had started just last week and she always loved coming back to Charleston, where she'd spent a good deal of her childhood with her favorite aunt both before and after her mother died.

And there was still the matter of Aunt Tildy's missing necklace and her mysterious gentleman friend. Was there a connection between the two? That definitely bore looking into.

She was trying to decide what to do until her aunt returned from the police station when her eye was caught by the array of round black buzzers that lined the side of the shop door. Doorbells. Next to each of them was a small hand-painted ceramic label.

"Oh, for goodness' sake," she murmured with a chuckle. She'd almost forgotten about those. Meant for Aunt Tildy's after-hours tarot customers, all of them rang a different note on the bell in her apartment. The thing was, they were the only buzzers, so all visitors, even family and friends, had to use them. And ever since she was a child, Seri could never decide which one to press.

She read over the choices on offer today.

The first one said, Press me if you're feeling blue. That one had always been popular. Especially when she was little and wanted an infusion of her aunt's famous chocolate-chip-and-secret-ingredient cookies. She'd never found out what the secret ingredient was back then, and nowadays she was afraid to ask. After all, Aunt Tildy still drove a VW bus decorated with big, bright flowers….

The second button read, Press me if your goal is fame and fortune. That one had been Seri's favorite during her college years. Ha. She was now a high school science teacher with no Nobel Prize in sight. 'Nuff said.

The next buzzer declared, Press me if you seek to find happiness and true love. She let out a soft snort. *Don't think so.* Aunt Tildy always said that true love was written in the stars. But in Seri's experience true love was about as likely as Tildy's alien prince being real. Despite the terminally bad example her commitment-phobic, largely absent father had set for her, she had experimented with the male species in college. Lord, what a colossal waste of time! She'd got a bigger bang from her science experiments, with far fewer side effects. She might have pressed that buzzer a few times in high school, but now? Not a chance.

The fourth one stated, Press me if revenge or protection is your greatest wish. Yeah, that one had always mystified her. Well, other than the time in the seventh grade when Ashley Hendrick stole the plans to her baking-soda-powered booster rocket and won the science fair with it. She probably wouldn't have said no if someone had offered to blast Ashley into outer space after that. Heaven protect her from cheats and liars.

The fifth and last buzzer was labeled, Press me if you long to be reunited with the one you loved and lost.

Whoa. That was new.

Occasionally Tildy changed up the labels, just to keep visitors on their toes. But rarely did a completely new one appear. Usually only when Tildy herself was going through some sort of mini-crisis. Having her treasured necklace stolen probably qualified. Seri just prayed her aunt wasn't once again mooning over the "alien prince" who had given it to her.

Stifling an uncharitable growl—okay, maybe revenge wasn't *such* a strange concept—she was grateful she didn't have to press a buzzer at the moment. She really hated that Aunt Tildy made you choose. As a teacher, Seri always gave her students the option of "none of the above" on tests.

With a self-deprecating sigh, she shook her head. God, why did she always, even now as an adult, think of this stupid buzzer thing as a test? Why did she always take it so damned seriously?

"Didn't find a choice you like?" a deep voice said from behind her.

Startled, she swung around to see a tall figure sprawled negligently on the carved wooden garden bench in the middle of the courtyard, observing her.

And it was decidedly *not* Aunt Tildy.

Seri swallowed a gasp of surprise…then a gasp of something quite different.

Good grief. This male was—objectively speaking—*gorgeous*. Nothing like the dull, insipid specimens she'd met in college.

Tanned and broad-shouldered, his body was muscular, his face lean, expressive and angular, with a definite air of authority. Hair the color of gold dust was just a little too long to be truly civilized. And his smile…the only way to describe it was *knowing*. She didn't usually go in for blond men, but this one… Lord, can you say "bad boy"?

"I—I, um…" Had he asked her a question?

That knowing smile curved up ever so slightly. "I take it you're *not* looking for love?"

She straightened. "Excuse me?"

He rose to his feet in a lithe movement that seemed to make the air around him shimmer. "The doorbells."

"Oh," she said, squinting at the odd optical illusion. But it had vanished. Strange.

He gazed at her expectantly.

Right. The doorbells. She forced herself to look at them, struggling to gather her badly scattered wits. Something about this man rattled her to the core. A feeling… *No, I don't do feelings*. An aura, then… *God, even worse.*

"What can I say?" She managed a weak laugh and glanced back at him, startled to find he was standing right behind her. "There are never enough choices."

His smile curved even more. "Never the *right* one," he agreed, tilting his head. "I'll bet I can guess, though."

"Oh, really?" At the moment she wasn't even sure *she* knew what the right one would be.

Her breath stalled as he reached for her—that is, *past* her, and opened the door to the Second Sun.

"You came for a reading? Tildy isn't here at the moment, but I'll do one for you." Then, as though he were a mind-reader instead of a tarot card reader, he added, "I can tell you all sorts of things you don't know."

"I…I'm not—" she stammered like an idiot, taking in the unlocked door with an inkling of suspicion. "You *work* here?"

"Not exactly." He motioned her in first, and she fully intended to refuse, but strangely, when he put his fingers lightly on the small of her back, a tingle shivered through her whole body and in that dizzy sensation she completely forgot her objections to being alone with him.

He followed her inside. "I pitch in whenever Tildy needs a hand. I own the bookstore." He jabbed a thumb at the Old World Rare and Antique Bookstore on the street side of the courtyard. "But I have a manager to watch things for me. Carch Sunstryker—" he introduced himself with a disarming smile "—at your service."

She was still recovering from that touch on her back, so when he extended his hand she really didn't want to risk touching him a second time, but for some reason her body was not obeying her today.

She put her hand in his, and was saying, "Seri Woodson," when sure enough that tingly sensation quivered straight through her again, knocking the polite, "Nice to meet you," right out of her mouth and leaving her more than a bit shaken. And stirred, too, for that matter.

"Ah," he said, giving her another bone-melting smile. "Serenity June. Tildy's niece."

She didn't know what was happening to her, but whatever it was, she didn't care for it. With a concerted effort, she withdrew her hand from his before she did something monumentally stupid. Like melt in a puddle at his feet.

This was ridiculous. She didn't do simpering, eyelash-batting female. She didn't do *men,* for crying out loud. *Remember the college experiments!*

"Just Seri," she corrected briskly, and tucked her hands under her armpits, safely out of danger. "Any idea when my aunt will be back?"

For a moment he gazed at her with that annoyingly knowing smile on his perfectly sculpted lips, then he pursed them as though trying to decide…lord knew what.

"Soon," he finally said. "But for now—" He swept his

hand toward the back room where Tildy's tarot table was set up behind a theatrical black velvet curtain. "Shall we?"

Alarm sifted through her. "Shall we what?"

But he just smiled.

Chapter 2

The woman was trouble.

And Carch Sunstryker, royal prince of Galifrax and intergalactic explorer, knew trouble when he saw it.

But with Serenity June Woodson, he'd actually *felt* it. Devils of Taron, how he'd felt the trouble brewing in her touch—on so many levels it made his head spin.

Yet another complication he did not need right now.

Damn, he hated this planet.

The top-secret mission that had brought him to this primitive, godforsaken world had seemed simple enough when his grandfather begged him to take it on. Land, locate the Imperial Star of the House of Sunstryker and get off-planet quickly, before anyone noticed anything unusual going on.

He'd only been here for three weeks, but obviously someone had noticed.

Now the Imperial Star, the sacred Galifracian treasure,

was gone. Vanished. And Carch was up the proverbial wormhole.

Did the young woman gazing up at him so uneasily have something to do with the powerful necklace's disappearance? Her showing up the day after it went missing could not be a coincidence. Was it merely familial solidarity, or something more sinister that had brought her to Charleston? He needed to find out.

"Well, what's it to be?" he asked, striving for relaxed conviviality when what he really wanted to do was grab her arms, stare straight into her eyes and probe her consciousness like a Lycean minesweeper.

Unfortunately, his skills weren't quite up to that. Besides, he didn't want her knowing about his unusual abilities. Or even suspecting. He didn't want *anyone* suspecting. Because that could have the even worse complication of possibly getting him dead.

And if he were killed before completing this mission, his family would very probably die, too. Executed one by one, starting with his grandfather, King Derrik.

So Carch pressed his teeth together in a smile and waited for her answer while, for the hundredth time, he mentally berated himself. Why the *hell* had he not stolen the blasted necklace back from Tildy Woodson as soon as he'd arrived on Earth three weeks ago, while he'd still had the chance?

Because he was a soft touch, that's why. He'd felt sorry for the nice old lady and ordered a duplicate to be made by a local artisan so she wouldn't be saddened by its loss. Apparently she had worn it faithfully since the night his grandfather had placed it around her neck, supposedly as a token of his everlasting love.

Love.

Carch barely resisted rolling his eyes. What could the man

have been *thinking,* risking a sentence of treason for a woman? And an *Earth* woman, at that!

"Maybe we should skip the reading," Tildy's niece said, bringing him rudely back to his present predicament. "I, uh, don't really believe in tarot and that kind of stuff." She shrugged apologetically.

He gave her what he hoped was a disarming grin. "Neither do I."

Tarot cards were such an archaic device. But a reading would provide good cover for touching her, which unfortunately was necessary for him to get into her head. Unless maybe…

"Is there, perhaps, something else you'd enjoy doing while we wait for Tildy?" He lifted his brows in not-so-veiled suggestion.

She blanched. He smiled again. And strolled after her as she made a beeline for the tarot table, saying, "A reading would be fine."

Yeah, he thought so. Not that he'd object to a more intimate kind of touching. That would no doubt be extremely pleasant. She was a pretty thing. Thick red-blond hair, a pleasant face and clear, intelligent green eyes. She had a very nice body. Tall and slim, but with those wonderful female curves in all the right places. Under her pretty, pleasingly short sundress, her legs were long, shapely and nicely toned. And her backside. Sweet and round, just beckoning to be—

Devils of Taron.

Mind on your mission, Sunstryker. Getting distracted by a sweet backside was probably exactly how his grandfather had landed in this mess in the first place.

Carch cooled his overactive jets while the object of his misguided hormones picked her chair.

For her readings, Tildy had very cleverly arranged four velvet armchairs, each one in a different color—deep blue, midnight purple, golden yellow and bloodred—around a small satin-draped table. Between the doorbells and the chair colors, Tildy would have a pretty good idea of the state of mind of her tarot customers and what they wanted to hear. The Imperial Star necklace would then do the rest, though she had no idea about that part. An effective combination. It was no wonder Tildy did well in her trade. A shame he had to take the necklace away from her.

When he found it, he reminded himself sternly.

Seri chose the red chair. Red, like the rich highlights in her autumn-honey hair. He drew the black velvet curtain closed across the double doorway that divided the tiny parlor from the rest of the New Age shop, trying not to think about how he'd always been partial to tresses the color of a Frithian sunset, all red and gold mingled in a tangle of loveliness. With the curtain pulled, the room was semi-dark, save for the rosy glow from a lava lamp sitting on a table in the corner.

"Perhaps a bit more light?" he asked, and lit several of the aromatic candles Tildy had scattered about, which sent the exotic smell of patchouli wafting through the air.

He hoped Tildy's signature fragrance would help calm Seri's nerves. Her anxiety was palpable as he took a seat in the yellow chair across from her. *Anxiety from guilt?*

He must tread lightly here. But he needed to find out more about her. Because of what he had seen in her mind in the brief glimpse he'd been allowed.

He'd sensed that, guilty or no, she was here today because of the necklace—and his grandfather.

And *that* was why she was trouble.

Aside from her sweet, round backside…

He went over to an antique library case and fetched Tildy's sandalwood box of tarot cards, setting it on the table between them.

"First you'll need to select a deck," he said, undoing the clasp of the beautifully carved box. "One that calls to you."

This time *her* brow went up.

"Very well, one that appeals to you," he amended dryly, opening the case to reveal eight different tarot decks tucked into velvet pockets.

Tildy had once explained the differences between them, but they were just pretty pictures to him. What he really needed to do was touch Seri long enough to roll her mind and harvest what useful feelings he found there. It was a nebular pain he wasn't able to see her mind clearly, or better yet, shapeshift his own appearance so he looked like her aunt, fooling her until he learned what he needed. Both of which he could have done with ease if he'd been of pure Galifracian blood, as were his father and grandfather.

However, one worked with those abilities one possessed. Being half human had its occasional disadvantages, but it had also allowed him to blend in like a native here on Earth with minimal effort. His Fracian body was already very similar, so it only took small changes to pass for human.

Seri hesitated over the tarot decks, seemingly torn between two.

"Pick them up," he urged, anxious to get this over with. "One in each palm."

She did, and he moved his hands under hers, lightly cupping them. As soon as their skins brushed, her breath gave a quick hitch and she yanked her hands away. But not before he was hit with a wave of her confused emotions: reluctance, trepidation, suspicion…and under it all, a pull of attraction that nearly took *his* breath away.

As an empath, Carch had experienced a variety of reactions from his subjects. And as a man, his effect on women was always favorable and persuasive. Using his gift of sensing emotions gave him a natural advantage. He knew what a female wanted before she asked—sometimes before she even knew herself. They usually loved that about him.

But this woman was different. This one did not want any part of him—certainly not *that* part. And yet, she seemed strangely compelled by his physical presence. They had an undeniably powerful carnal attraction. But rather than explore it to their mutual satisfaction, he sensed she wanted nothing more than to run away from it, from him.

This he could use.

"Why don't we try this one?" he suggested, taking the decks that were about to slip from her fingers and selecting one for her. She nodded and her hands disappeared into her lap.

"Relax," he said lightly. "I promise not to say anything bad. This is supposed to be fun, right?"

"If you say so." Finally an uneasy smile formed on her lips.

Lips, he couldn't help noticing, that were pink and full and curved just so. A potent wisp of desire curled through his gut as he watched them part a fraction.

He jerked his gaze up. *Mind on your mission, Sunstryker,* he reminded himself for the second time.

He shuffled the cards, then set them on the table. "Cut, please." She did, then he laid the cards out into a Celtic cross just as Tildy had shown him. He hadn't a clue what the cards meant that he turned face-up, but that didn't worry him too much.

"Put your fingertips on the center card," he instructed.

She looked up at him, surprised. "Why?"

"It's how I do readings." He tapped the card.

Reluctantly, she did as he instructed, and he swiftly put the tips of his own fingers on the card as well, so they just touched hers. When she startled and tried to move away he grasped her hands, suddenly impatient.

"Don't," he warned in low tones, capturing her gaze.

She froze, looking as though she wanted to bolt. But her mind was suddenly open and vulnerable. He probed ruthlessly and she shivered; she wanted to look away but he wouldn't let her.

Easy, man. No need to scare the girl.

He gathered himself and soothed her skittishness as he would a virgin, more than pleased when her skin flushed with heat and goose bumps.

"Don't be afraid," he whispered. "I won't hurt you."

He could feel her denial of him, her confused refusal to accept his presence in her head. He ignored her ineffectual efforts to expel him and peered deeper. If she had been less afraid she could have shielded her thoughts and feelings from him. His skill was far from all-seeing. He could only sense the emotions his subject did not consciously hide from him.

In this case, she hid very little. He could feel her concern for the necklace, mixed with worry over her aunt and…a more hidden fear of…something he couldn't see. He found nothing malicious within her thoughts. But suddenly it didn't matter because of…the most incredible desire that swept over him to…kiss her.

All he could think of was how luscious her mouth would feel pressed against his.

Why not? What could it hurt?

"I predict," he murmured, reverting to simple tarot reader, "that a golden-haired stranger is about to come into your life."

Under the tiny round table he squeezed his knees together, trapping hers between them as he tugged on her hands to bring her closer. She sucked in a breath, eyes widening as his intention became clear.

He slid his fingers behind her neck, encouraging her to close the few inches that remained between their lips.

Tentatively, sweetly, her lashes lowered and she leaned

toward him. Her tantalizing woman's scent wreathed its way through his consciousness. Tempting him. Making him forget all about the necklace and his mission. Making him forget about everything but possessing her as soon as possible.

"And I predict," he whispered, "that he will take you places you've never dreamed existed."

Her lips were nearly to his when suddenly the velvet curtain whisked apart and a cheerful voice sang out, "Oh, there you are, my dear!"

"Aunt Tildy!" Seri snapped back in her chair so fast Carch feared she might get whiplash.

"Serenity, darling!" her aunt exclaimed. "What in the world are you doing here?" Thankfully oblivious to the undercurrents, Tildy rushed over and gave her niece a big hug as she shot to her feet. "I see you've already met my friend Carch."

"Um…yes." Flustered, Seri wouldn't meet his eyes.

"Oh, sweetheart, can you believe it? Isn't it just too exciting?" the older woman gushed.

"What is, Aunt Tildy?"

"After all this time. Just imagine! He sent his own grandson to find me!"

A hint of wariness flitted across Seri's face. "Grandson? Who are you talking about, Aunt Tildy?"

"Why, the love of my life, Derrik Sunstryker, of course!"

The younger woman's eyes narrowed, and the brief scowl she shot Carch nearly singed his eyelashes. "You mean the—the man who gave you the missing necklace?" she asked suspiciously.

Carch braced himself. He didn't need to be an empath to know what was coming next.

Tildy nodded enthusiastically. "That's right, dear. Prince Carch has come to visit us from the planet Galifrax, all the way on the other side of the Milky Way!"

Chapter 3

The planet *Galifrax?*

Oh. My. God.

Seri blinked at her beloved aunt and tried not to let the dismay show on her face. Or the anger. Slowly she turned to My Favorite Martian, who stood with a pleasant but inscrutable expression on his own. Funny, he didn't look the least bit little or green, and there was not an antenna in sight.

"Indeed," Seri said. "The Milky Way."

"No, the other side—" Aunt Tildy started to say, then clapped her hands over her mouth and looked contritely at Carch Sunstryker—or whoever the hell he really was. "Oh! I'm so sorry! I was supposed to keep that a secret, wasn't I?"

"I'll just bet you were," Seri muttered.

"It's all right, Tildy," the Martian said, completely unruffled. "No harm done."

"She won't tell anyone, I promise. Will you, my dear?" Her

aunt turned appealing eyes to Seri and lowered her voice conspiratorially. "If the government found out…Well, you can just imagine what would happen to the poor boy."

Yeah. Like maybe he'd go to jail, where the unscrupulous charlatan belonged. But she didn't say that. He'd obviously endeared himself to Aunt Tildy, so Seri should play nice until she found out exactly what he was up to.

"Yes," she agreed, unable to completely stifle the sarcasm. "I certainly can imagine what would happen to him." She crossed her arms. "So, what might a guy from outer space—a *prince* no less—be doing here on our humble planet?"

A muscle twitched above his cheek, but it was Aunt Tildy who answered triumphantly, "Carch's grandfather sent him to check on me." The bangles on her arms tinkled melodiously as her faded blue eyes twinkled with joy. "To make sure I'm doing well."

Seri nearly choked on that one. "You mean—"

"Yes! Derrik. The handsome prince from another world I fell in love with all those years ago!" Her aunt smiled happily, glancing back and forth between them as though things simply couldn't be more perfect. "Isn't it wonderful?"

Carch cleared his throat and said, "Actually, I'm sure you two have lots of things to catch up on. Family things and such. I should leave you to talk."

"Oh, no," Seri protested, holding a hand up. Like she'd really let him escape before nailing his hide to the wall. "That can wait. You must join us for lunch. Really, I'd love to learn more about you and your…planet."

Aunt Tildy clapped her hands. "Oh, what a splendid idea. I'll just run upstairs and throw something together. Carch, dear, why don't you show Seri the changes we've made to the salon, and then wander up in a few minutes?" Then she rushed off and disappeared up the staircase that led to her apartment, leaving Seri and Carch staring at each other.

"What the hell do you think you're up to?" Seri demanded as soon as her aunt was out of earshot.

Carch took a half step toward her, and once again the air around him seemed to shimmer. She blinked away the illusion, only to find him reaching for her arm. She jumped back.

"Don't touch me!"

Strange things happened to her when he touched her. She'd think later about how he managed his insidious magic, but right now she didn't want the man's body anywhere near hers.

"I'd just like to point out," he said, following her into the cozy, sweet-scented shop area, "that *I* never said I was from another planet."

She turned to him accusingly. "No, because it was supposed to be a big secret. Right?"

His lips curved in a wry smile. "How would you have handled it? Being a space alien is not exactly the kind of rumor I want going around about me."

"So you're saying you're *not* from outer space?"

His smile turned indulgent. "Do you believe in extraterrestrials?"

"Of course not. At least…certainly not ones that land on Earth trying to con old ladies."

"I'm not trying to con your aunt, Seri. But the last thing I want is to crush a nice old lady's cherished memories." He stepped closer, looking oh, so sincere. "Please, can't we call a truce?"

The very innocence of his expression made Seri even more suspicious. "Who are you? Really?"

"I told you the truth. I really am Carch Sunstryker and I own the bookstore on the other side of the courtyard."

"Unusual name," she said. Alien or no, Derrik Sunstryker

was the name of the man who Aunt Tildy had always insisted gave her the necklace that was now missing. That could absolutely not be a coincidence. The Martian *had* to be up to no good.

"Yes, my name is unusual," he admitted, and tipped his head to one side. "You still don't believe me, do you?"

"I know you're after my aunt's necklace," she said. "Why?"

His expression didn't change an iota, not so much as a twitch. But something shifted in the air between them. If she'd had her science lab equipment, she was sure she'd be able to measure the sudden tension arcing around them.

"I promised Tildy I'd help her find her necklace," he said.

"Are you sure you don't already have it?" Seri asked evenly.

"I wish to God I did," he murmured.

That she believed. It had to be incredibly valuable. Though Aunt Tildy had never had it appraised, Seri would be surprised if the gem-encrusted solid-gold star wasn't worth a small fortune. Bookstores couldn't be all that profitable…. Had he somehow found out about her aunt's mythical prince and spun a story to get his hands on it?

"I know you're worried about your aunt," he said, startling her because again he was standing right in front of her. "Can't we put aside this whole spaceman thing and work together to find her necklace?"

Seri looked up, suddenly noticing how tall he was. How *really* tall he was. She was by no means a short woman, yet he towered over her by a good six or more inches. She actually had to crane her neck to see his eyes. Surely he hadn't been this tall outside in the garden? Or his shoulders quite so broad….

"That way, you'll see I mean your aunt no harm," he continued. "Nor you. I'm just a simple bookstore owner doing a favor for a friend."

On the contrary, there was nothing simple about him.

She realized with a shock that he was coming closer. And closer. For the life of her she couldn't make her feet move away. He reached for her and she held her breath anxiously, unable to avoid the brush of his fingers over her hands.

Instantly, she felt the low thrum of…something…some kind of weird energy…purl through her whole being. There was no other way to describe it other than that she felt an overwhelming presence—his presence—flow around her like a warm tidal wave, leaving her thoughts scattered and dizzy. She sensed him move closer still, so their bodies touched, but she could do nothing to stop him, or even to protest. But oh, lord, she didn't *want* to protest. She wanted to melt into him, to feel him all around her like the warm, comforting sea. She wanted him to kiss her.

Their desires mingled, and his lips came down on hers. Her body shivered clear down to her toes as the feel of his kiss streaked through her like a sensory aurora borealis. His sigh was soft and his body hard, and he tasted…oh, sweet mercy, he tasted so good!

His fingers slid into her hair and held her head immobile while he deepened their kiss. Not that she would pull away for all the world. His tongue dipped into her mouth and playfully teased hers.

"Open to me," his voice whispered through her mind. He pulled her tight against him and it was like diving into a turbulent body of hot, tingling water. Only his arms around her kept her from drowning in his fathomless, shimmering depths.

Ohmigod, it's happening again. Those strange feelings.

This was... She was…

Oh, no, what am I doing?

It took all her willpower, but she managed to drag her mouth from his. "Wait," she gasped, clutching his arms and pushing him away. "Stop."

He lifted, and peered down at her as though he, too, had been lost in something he didn't quite understand.

She shook off the aftereffects of the unfamiliar and mortifyingly potent sexual desire his kiss had produced. What was wrong with her? She took a steadying breath as he stepped back from her with a frown.

"I—I'm sorry. I don't—"

Just then, Aunt Tildy's voice sang out, "Lunch is ready!" and her head popped into view above the staircase baluster. "Come and get it!"

Seri wasn't sure if she could move. She was too shell-shocked to do anything but pray Carch hadn't started unbuttoning her blouse.

Apparently Martians recovered their composure faster than Earthlings. He calmly grabbed her hand and pulled her toward the staircase. "Be right up," he called as though unaffected by what had just happened.

She managed to stumble after him up the narrow flight of stairs into Aunt Tildy's living room. On an ornate elephant-foot coffee table in front of a plush loveseat, Tildy had laid out a huge brass tray loaded with sandwiches, tea things and a even a plate of small dessert cakes.

"Sit, sit!" Aunt Tildy said, fussing with the cups and saucers. "So, I trust you two have gotten better acquainted?"

Seri wanted to crawl under the table and hide the way she used to when she was a kid. How her aunt made a living reading tarot was a pure mystery. Her obliviousness was blinding.

But Carch just smiled cheerfully. "We certainly have. And we have some good news for you, too."

"Oh?" Her aunt looked up at them expectantly.

"Really?" Seri blurted out before she could stop herself. *What news?*

"Yes," said Carch, giving her another of his obnoxiously

knowing smiles. "Seri and I have agreed to work together to find your necklace. Until it's safely back in your hands, we won't be leaving each other's side."

Chapter 4

Carch felt at least a trickle of satisfaction.

He'd blown it. He'd blown it big-time. But he'd nevertheless managed to salvage the situation nicely.

"Excellent!" Tildy said in response to his statement, beaming at him and Seri as she poured tea. "I'll confess I was quite worried, leaving the fate of my precious necklace in the hands of the police. They didn't seem to take me seriously for some reason."

Carch sent Seri a confident wink. She wouldn't dare contradict him about their working together, for fear he'd reveal to her aunt what she'd just been doing. *Kissing a perfect stranger.* He'd read her mortification over that even as he'd kissed her. Silly to be so embarrassed over something that felt so incredibly good.

Not that he wasn't grateful for her blushes. Otherwise, she was just contrary enough, she might have balked at being maneuvered like this. And the cold fact was, he needed to keep her within his grasp. After searching her mind he was no longer wary of her motives for coming to Charleston. But she still suspected him of nefarious intentions, and that could easily lead to disaster if he didn't watch her closely.

Ah, well. No law said he couldn't enjoy himself while protecting his identity and fulfilling his duty to the king. If kissing her again would ensure the outcome of his mission, he'd just have to man-up.

"Working together will be our pleasure," he told Tildy, deciding this wasn't such a bad turn of events, after all.

"Of course," Seri interjected, glaring at him, "the part about not leaving each other's side was an exaggeration."

Yeah, well, they'd see about that.

He sat down next to Seri on the loveseat—she didn't like it, but there wasn't another free chair in the tiny living room. She went out of her way not to let her thigh touch his. Fine. There'd be plenty of time for that when they were alone again. So he relaxed and enjoyed the delicious meal while Tildy chatted on about who might have taken the Imperial Star, and why.

"I just know it was that Madam Clarissa," she said, frowning.

"The lady with the palmistry shop at the other end of the courtyard?" Seri asked, surprised.

"Clarissa has always been jealous of my customers," Tildy confided with a nod. "She's constantly dreaming up ways to steal business from me."

"How would this help?" Carch asked. The whole concept of a market society driven by money was foreign to him. Galifrax itself had long since abandoned the divisive, antiquated system of monetary barter, recognizing that greed for wealth was the undisputed source of most of the conflict and contention across the galaxies.

"By distracting me so I can't concentrate on my readings,"

Tildy explained. "If I can't give my customers a good tarot reading, they'll try Clarissa's palmistry instead."

"Well, I can't imagine anyone on the courtyard could be the thief," Seri said. Her cup paused halfway to her mouth. "Except…weren't the owners of the Thin Man Gallery involved in some shady business a few years back? Arrested and everything?"

Carch perked up. What was this?

"David and Alan," Tildy clarified. "Well, yes, but those charges were eventually dropped." She shook her head. "And it couldn't be them. They bring me brownies. And send me postcards from their buying trips. Heavens no, it can't be them."

"What kind of shady business?" Carch asked, reaching over to nab the last chocolate chip cookie from Seri's plate. She'd just beaten him to it, and he was particularly partial to them.

"Something about forged provenance papers on one of their Art Deco pieces." Tildy waved a dismissive hand and her bangles tinkled. "But it was all just a mix-up."

Seri snagged the cookie back just as he opened his mouth to take a bite. "That was a necklace, too, as I recall," she said, making a face at him as she downed the cookie with great relish.

Smart aleck.

His lips parted involuntarily as her tongue slid out to gather a stray morsel of chocolate from her own lip. He forced himself to look away. "I know you've searched everywhere, Tildy, but perhaps Seri and I should reinspect the shop and your apartment thoroughly before accusing anyone?"

He wouldn't put it beyond Tildy to have dropped or misplaced it somewhere right under their noses. She was endearing, but more than a little absent-minded.

"Well, I have already reported it to the police," she reminded him. "They're bound to investigate."

Which was another thing he was more than uneasy about. He'd done his best to stop her going, but she'd been adamant this morning. Luckily, they hadn't seemed to treat it as a priority.

"Then we'll save them the trouble of conducting their own search," he said. The last thing he wanted anywhere near him was any brand of law enforcement. A simple background check could lead to some very awkward questioning. Or far worse.

Seri was gazing at him consideringly. Still suspicious. A spurt of impatience rocketed through him. Dammit, why wasn't she like all the other women he'd met on this planet—a sucker for his looks and charm, able to be influenced by a single brush of his fingers? Gods of Moradth, Seri's intransigence reminded him all too well of his mother back home. It really was too annoying.

He gave the object of his present annoyance a practiced smile. "Which would you rather search, the shop or the apartment?"

"Oh, definitely the apartment," she said, then glanced down at her pretty dress. It was short and slim in a light shade of blue-green. "But first I want to change. I'd better get my things and unpack. I was in a hurry and left my suitcase in the car."

Tildy's face drained of color and a look of consternation swept over her normally serene features. "Oh, dear."

"What is it?" Seri asked, and Carch leaned back on the sofa, trying not to grin. Ah, yes. He'd forgotten all about that....

"Sweetheart, do you remember when I phoned last night about the necklace, how I said you really didn't need to come to Charleston to help find it?"

Seri nodded slowly. "But I knew you needed me. How could I not come after all you've done for me?"

"Oh, dear," Tildy repeated, and leaned over to give her niece a hug. "You are such a good girl. I should have known, and told you—"

"Told me what, Aunt Tildy?" she asked, starting to become visibly alarmed.

"Your room. I'm having it remodeled."

Seri looked nonplussed. "Remodeled?"

"The hardwood was in deplorable shape, and remember that huge crack in the wall? The work was supposed to have been finished by now, you understand, because I'd hoped you'd come visit this summer, but Bob—the carpenter—well, he sprained his wrist last week." Tildy nibbled her lip.

"And?"

"And it's still all torn up. There's no way you can stay in that room. There's no plaster on the walls, and the floor is covered in sawdust and old nails!"

It took Seri but a second to shake off her surprise, and shrug. "No matter. I'll sleep on the loveseat out here."

Tildy looked scandalized. "Of course you can't! It's far too short for you!" Her eyes sought Carch's in appeal, and he smiled as though he hadn't a clue. No way was he going to be the one to suggest what was coming.

"Then I'll sleep on the floor," Seri said decisively.

He continued to smile as Tildy said, "Over my dead body. Carch, dear, you have loads of space. Couldn't she stay with you?"

Seri actually gasped.

"Absolutely," he gracefully conceded, inwardly rubbing his hands in triumph. Talk about keeping her close. He couldn't have planned it better if he'd tried. "She can take one of the guest rooms."

"Splendid," Tildy said, slapping her palms against her knees and then rising to clear away the tea things amidst the jingle of silver and a cloud of patchouli. "Then it's all settled."

Seri's mouth was still opening and closing. "No!" she finally got out. "I can't stay with him! I—I barely know him!"

"Well, I know him, darling, and there's absolutely nothing to worry about. Carch Sunstryker is a perfect gentleman.

Besides—" she sent him a gentle warning look "—he knows he has me to answer to."

He'd risen from the loveseat when Tildy stood, and now he gave her a little bow. "I promise to continue being the perfect gentleman I've always been," he assured her.

Seri snorted under her breath.

He gave her a wink.

Her chin rose, but before she could say anything, he cut her off by glancing at his watch. "Why don't we get started with the search so there'll still be time to hit the pawn shops this afternoon?" he suggested. "That is, if we don't find the necklace."

She clamped her jaws together, but gave a reluctant nod. "All right. We can talk about the other thing later."

He didn't argue. Hell, she could talk all she liked. But between him and Aunt Tildy she didn't stand a chance of resisting.

Whether she liked it or not, she was spending the night with him. Which should give him ample opportunity to take care of her inconvenient suspicions. And even, perchance, to find a common ground they'd both enjoy....

The search did not turn up the necklace.

While Tildy attended to customers in the shop, Seri scoured every square inch of Aunt Tildy's apartment. No luck. When she went downstairs to help Carch, he was just finishing up one last corner. Judging by the way he was concentrating on the task of sifting through the hundreds of books, the shelves of tarot paraphernalia, the cases filled with crystals, incense and scores of New Age doodads her aunt had crammed into the overflowing shop, Seri didn't think even a dead palmetto bug could have escaped his notice.

The customers, however—all female—did notice him. Seri felt an unexpected and totally inappropriate surge of jealousy when she saw that every woman in the place was agog. To his credit, he appeared not to notice them in return. In fact, he was concentrating so single-mindedly on his search, he didn't see her quietly enter the room. Which gave her a chance to observe him in action.

Okay, she really couldn't blame the other women. Sweet mercy, he was a gorgeous man. Though, perhaps not in the classic sense. Carch Sunstryker was tall, broad and golden as a pagan god, but his face was a touch too weathered, his gaze a tad too sharp, his features a trace too chiseled to be strictly handsome. He exuded an aura of utter confidence and authority which would exclude him from the harmless kind of male beauty that might grace a magazine cover. Except maybe *Mercenary Monthly* or the like.

But for Seri, he was exactly the kind of man she'd always been attracted to.

And because of that, the kind she had always avoided. Because he was exactly the kind of man a woman had no chance of ever controlling. And control was essential in life. Control was necessary to be master of one's own fate, to choose one's own path rather than to have it chosen for you. Bad things happened when one lost control.

Though heaven knew she had already lost control with Carch Sunstryker. How on earth had he managed to sweep her into his arms yet again? Every time he touched her, she seemed to lose all willpower to resist him. Very disturbing. Too bad it felt so incredibly good. Which was even more disturbing.

"You checking out my butt?" he asked without turning, bent over examining a low shelf of imported Indian perfumes.

She started, but managed to say, "Don't flatter yourself. I haven't the slightest interest—"

"Sure you don't, angel." When he turned to stand, that insufferably knowing smile was on his lips again. "Any luck upstairs?"

She frowned. "The name is Seri, and no. I scoured the apartment from top to bottom, but didn't find a sign of the necklace."

"Me neither." He brushed his hands together, his smile fading. "I was really hoping…" He shook his head, looking more concerned than he should be over something that wasn't his. "Guess we'd better make a list of pawn shops."

"Why do you care so much?" she asked bluntly. Aunt Tildy might trust him, but she didn't. There was something going on. Something he was hiding from her. And from Aunt Tildy. She aimed to find out what it was.

"I made a promise," was all he said. But the determined look in his crystalline-blue eyes sent a shiver down her spine. And suddenly she was very glad she wasn't on the wrong side of that promise.

Or…was she? Now there was a scary thought.

"Carch—"

"About those pawn shops. I found a phone book where we can look up addresses," he interrupted, pointing. "It's by the cash register."

She let his motivation go for now. He was right. Their first priority was just to find the necklace. After that, it would soon become apparent if he had plans other than to return it to Tildy.

She wondered if she should let the police know of her suspicions. Let *them* check out his background. That way she wouldn't be the bad guy and her aunt couldn't possibly be angry with her for questioning his character. It merited some thought.

Meanwhile, she grabbed the phone book, pen and paper and began to copy down addresses. "Couldn't we just call the pawn shops?"

"We could, but I'd rather be there in person when we ask about the necklace."

"Why?"

"Easier to tell if they're lying," he said absently, then

finished inspecting the last of the shop's shelves. "Well, that's done. Not here." Disappointment colored his tone. "Let's hope we have better luck with the pawn shops."

She lifted the completed list in her hand. "There's over a dozen places. We'll never get to all of them in one afternoon."

"In that case, let's start with the closest and work our way out."

Which was exactly what they did.

Or…what they planned to do.

The first pawn shop was just a block away. Seri had high hopes for this one since it was so near the scene of the crime, and was also appropriately upscale because of the neighborhood. Unfortunately, none of the employees had seen anything like Aunt Tildy's necklace.

After chatting for a few minutes with the owner, explaining to whom the necklace belonged and where it had disappeared, Carch handed the owner a business card. "If you hear anything about it, anything at all, give me a call. There's a ten-thousand-dollar reward for its return. No questions asked."

Seri's jaw dropped in shock. She stared at him, speechless, as he squired her from the shop. Ten thousand dollars! Good lord! So many questions flitted through her mind she couldn't think which one to ask first.

"Where's your car parked?" he asked as though nothing out of the ordinary had just happened.

"In a garage on— My God, Carch, what were you—"

"A garage where? What street?"

"Queen. The other side of Meeting. But—"

He touched the small of her back, and she jumped as a tingly sensation shot through her. She hurried toward the exit so he wouldn't touch her again.

"Is it a rental?"

She nodded, shaking off the strange feeling. "Carch, about the—"

"We'll return it then. I have a perfectly good Mercedes we can use."

She stopped, digging in her heels on the sidewalk once they were outside the pawn shop, and narrowed a glare at him. "Ten thousand dollars? Are you crazy? You only met my aunt a few weeks ago. Why would you do that?"

His expression suffused with humor. "My grandfather would expect no less of me."

She ground her teeth. "Stop it. Your name is not Sunstryker and you are *not* from outer space. My aunt may be delusional, but I'm not."

He shrugged casually. "If you say so."

"I want an explanation. A rational one. Now."

He sighed and seemed to ponder for a moment. "What can I say? I like Tildy, and I have more money than I know what to do with. The trinket obviously means a lot to her. Why not make an old lady happy?"

Yeah, right. "To the tune of ten thousand dollars?"

He shrugged again. "Why not?"

Her mind churned as she started walking down the street. He was *rich?* That didn't exactly jibe with her theory of him being a thief or a con man.

Of course, she had no evidence he really was wealthy—or how he'd come by that wealth if he was—she reminded herself as she skirted around a homeless person who was shuffling along the middle of the sidewalk. She only had Carch's word there was money for a reward. Talk was cheap.

She tried to puzzle it out, finding and discarding theories that might possibly explain this unexpected turn of events.

Maybe the reason had something to do with his family. Maybe it really was his grandfather who'd—

Suddenly Carch's hand gripped her shoulder lightly, bringing her to a halt. A wave of living, physical awareness rolled from his hand around her body and up through her mind. Her confused thoughts fell away; suddenly all she wanted was to gaze up at him and let him convince her of his innocence.

His fingers lifted and the connection abruptly broke. Instantly her suspicions returned. She jerked away from him. Wow.

What *was* it about that man's touch? How did he *do* that? The scientist in her refused to believe what he made her feel was possible, but her body said otherwise.

"Which car's yours?" he asked.

She realized with a start that they were standing at the entrance to the parking garage. "It's on level three," she answered before thinking. Then hurriedly added, "But I really don't think it's a good idea—"

"Nonsense," he returned. "Rental cars are expensive, and I gather teachers don't exactly pull in the big bucks."

Now that was an understatement.

She had no concrete reason to say no, but nevertheless it was against her better judgment that she led him to the car, drove it to an agency office located a few blocks away and allowed him to load her suitcase into the taxi he'd called to take them to his Mercedes.

Which turned out to be at his place.

Where she was supposed to sleep tonight.

Ho boy.

When they got to his home just off the Battery, she stood on the manicured curb and gazed up at the three-story antebellum Georgian mansion where he lived. Good lord. It had to be worth several million. Even if he was renting, he had to be rolling in it to afford this palace.

Could he really be helping Aunt Tildy out of the goodness

of his heart, and not to get his hands on the valuable necklace? Carch Sunstryker obviously had no need for money.

"Shall we?" He gave her a smile, hefting her suitcase and motioning for her to precede him to the front door.

Or was there something else going on? To her mind, things just didn't add up. Sorry, Carch Sunstryker did not strike her as the good Samaritan type. If he wasn't a thief, surely there must be some *other* reason he wanted to get his hands on the necklace.

And she'd better figure out what it was before Aunt Tildy got hurt.

Which meant she had to go along with this little bedroom farce for now. So she could dig a little deeper.

She swallowed her consternation at the twist of fate that had landed her in this untenable situation. Untenable because he'd probably make another pass at her. Probably tonight. And she couldn't rebuff him outright or he wouldn't trust her with his secrets. But if she didn't, a single caress of his hand or brush of his lips would no doubt once again send her control spinning into oblivion.

And then she'd *really* be in trouble.

Giving her another of those annoyingly knowing smiles, he unlocked the door and pushed it open, bidding her enter his world.

Peering into the depths of the unknown, she hesitated. Maybe she should make one last bid for a hotel room, after all.

But she never got the chance.

A loud bang exploded. It reverberated like a gunshot off the buildings and echoed down the quiet street. Carch's eyes widened, then he looked down. So did she.

And gasped.

His chest was covered in blood.

Chapter 5

Moradth's minions. He'd been shot!

Carch stowed his incredulity for another time. He was fading fast, his life's blood pouring from the ragged, gaping wound in his chest. Mentally, he sought out the path of destruction the projectile had torn through his flesh and organs. It had nearly grazed his heart. *Fatal.*

He had to shift. *Now.* Or die.

Seri had already grabbed his arm or he'd be on the ground. He held on to her with a steely grip, gritted his teeth and ordered, "Get me inside. Quickly."

For once she didn't argue. She half lifted, half dragged him clinging to her like a monkey into the foyer and slammed the heavy door, locking it behind them.

"My God, Carch! I'm calling 911!"

"No," he gritted out with an effort, knitting his insides just enough to keep the organs working. "Safe for now." The assassin would know there was only one way to survive this kind of wound. He'd assume Carch was done for.

He might well be right. Carch could stave off the inevitable only a few minutes more before more drastic measures were required. Could he trust Seri? No choice. He had to risk it.

"Towel," he panted, darting a look at the powder room off the foyer. He released his grip on her and slid to the floor as she sprinted for a towel. She returned with a big fluffy one before he could shake the black spots from his vision.

"I don't care what you say, I'm calling an ambulance." She reached into her purse for her cell phone.

"No!" he commanded, gathering what was left of his strength for the coming ordeal. "No time. Staunch the bleeding. Hard. Please hurry," he added when she looked as though she'd mutiny. He grabbed her hand and pulled her down on the floor next to him, placing the towel over the hole in his chest. After a heartbeat's hesitation, she pressed it firmly onto the wound. It wouldn't do much, but every ounce of blood he kept could be the difference between life and death. "Good," he mumbled.

"Carch—"

"Listen to me, Seri," he rasped, battling to stay conscious. Already the black spots were spreading, invading the center of his vision. "You must…help. Promise, no matter what… you see…you won't move the towel away from the wound." If she did, his blood would gush and he'd be dead.

"Of course—"

"Swear it." Painfully, he turned his body so he lay face-down on the floor. The towel followed faithfully.

"I swear." He couldn't see her expression, but her tone said it all. She thought he was nuts and was ready to wrest control of the situation.

No time to lose.

He squeezed his eyes shut, gathered his swiftly waning powers and willed the process to begin. He started with his insides, the area torn apart by the unique Galifracian tri-bullet that was designed to inflict maximum damage and minimize the chances of being able to do just what he was attempting.

To shapeshift. Back to his native form.

And thereby reknit his flesh together as it had been originally designed, before it was too late.

"Close…your eyes," he ordered. Wanting to spare her. Knowing full well she would disobey.

He cried out as the process began. He was half human, so it was a difficult and painful procedure to change his entire body. Usually he only altered his outer appearance, with minimal effort or discomfort, as he had in order to blend in on Earth. But now he must shift his whole body, every molecule.

And he must trust Seri not to run screaming from the sight.

He was so weak, and growing weaker by the second. But bit by bit he managed to force the change upon himself. He was vaguely aware of his own muted cries as his insides dissolved and reformed anew, cursing his father for siring him on an Earth woman and thus condemning him to the need for this torture.

First the inside, then the outside of his body renewed itself in shuddering waves. The shifting seemed to go on forever, but in reality it was all over just ten minutes later. In a shallow puddle of blood from his original wound, Carch lay on the cool marble floor of his foyer, covered in sweat and gasping for breath. But healed. *Thank Moradth.*

"You can take the towel away now," he managed, and let himself relax.

Seri was unnaturally quiet. He felt the blood-soaked towel slip from under his body. She made a mewling noise. No doubt the towel held the alien bullet he had expelled from his flesh.

He let out a long breath. He really didn't want to have this confrontation. Especially now, when things had gotten exponentially more complicated. But again he had no choice. She must understand what they were facing, and what was at stake.

He rolled to his back, giving her a view of his natural body full-on.

Her hands flew to her mouth. To her credit, she didn't scream. But her eyes were wild with disbelief, terror barely held at bay.

No. Not terror, he realized. Fear, yes. But more than fear, they held incomprehension. Her world was being shaken to its very foundation.

Her gaze poured over him, took him in, every last detail. He knew he didn't look all that different from the Carch Sunstryker she'd known up until fifteen minutes ago. A little leaner, face shaped a little differently but similar enough to recognize most of his features. His skin would be glowing gold. That would be the greatest difference. And his feet weren't exactly human. But they were still safely enclosed in his shoes. Thank goodness for clothes. If she saw the front of his body naked she might really be scared.

She whimpered anyway.

"Angel," he murmured softly. For she truly was his guardian angel. "Don't be frightened. I'm not going to hurt you. Trust me."

Her eyes locked on to his. She was still fearful, but struggling to find a hold on reality, fighting to make sense of the impossibilities her vision was showing her.

She tentatively reached her hand toward him, then snatched it back. "Tell me I'm dreaming," she whispered hoarsely.

"Afraid not," he said, already starting to feel much better physically. Gingerly he sat up, putting a hand to his chest. Smooth and pristine. He let out a sigh. He hadn't shifted all that many times, and each time he did he was amazed it worked.

"You're— You're not— You're—" she stammered.

"Not human?" He gave her a lopsided smile. *Good girl.* She was coming round. Score one for the science teacher. "Yeah. I know."

Her fearful look was slowly morphing into one of cautious disbelief. "Oh, God. Aunt Tildy was right. All these years, everyone's been making fun of her…but she was right all along, wasn't she?"

This was going better than he'd expected. "Yep," he admitted with no small relief.

"You're from… You're from…"

"Galifrax. Moon to the second sun of Mercidia, in the galaxy of Erindoth in the Sargasso nebula."

"Beyond the Milky Way," she said in a strangled voice.

"Exactly." He held out his hand. "A pleasure to meet you, Earthling."

Inexplicably, her eyes filled with tears. She let out a half sob, half laugh, glanced warily at his hand, then reluctantly took it in hers. "Likewise," she said over a tremor. "I hope."

A sense of humor. Always a good sign. "Believe me," he assured her, squeezing her hand, "there are no plans for an invasion, of any kind."

She blew out a breath and stared at him doubtfully. "No Vogon constructor fleet?"

His brows flickered. "Huh?"

She shook her head and, with the barest trace of a smile, wiped her eyes. "Never mind." She looked at him, not exactly nervously, but not exactly at ease either. "So, spaceman, what do we do now?"

Her hand was still warm in his. He brought it to his lips. It only jerked a little. "I must say, you've taken this very well."

"An illusion. I'm still in shock. The real reaction will come later. Right after you tell me who's trying to kill you and what my aunt's necklace has to do with it."

Surprise swept through him, along with a new respect for the woman who was obviously fighting hard to keep it together and succeeding enough to actually put two and two together.

He briefly considered lying, denying it all. Then he sighed. Why bother? Serenity June Woodson was sharp as a Solutrian thorn tree. She'd find out the truth sooner or later. And the fact was, it would be helpful to have a confidant in his quest. An ally.

"I will tell you," he said, rising and pulling her to her feet at the same time. "But first I want to get cleaned up."

And try to figure out just how everything had gone to hell so far and so fast. In the space of twenty-four hours things had progressed from just peachy to bad, then to worse and now downright dangerous. To top it off, a native had found out he was from off-planet. A native who might actually be taken seriously.

Everyone knew the number-one rule of space travel: Never tell them you're an alien.

Damn.

Well, maybe a shower would clear his head and give him a clue about how to get out of this mess. He headed for the stairs, but at the bottom of the staircase Seri balked.

He looked down at their hands, still joined. She was trying her best to extract hers from his firm grip. "What?"

"Um, maybe you should go upstairs by yourself," she said.

"But your dress is covered in blood." Which reminded him. "We must have left your suitcase outside. I'll get it."

"But what about—"

He left before she could finish her sentence. When he returned, she took the hard case and clutched it nervously to her chest, almost like a shield. "I can't believe you went out there."

"I doubt the bastard hung around."

"You know who did this?"

"Not specifically, but I have an idea."

"Does he know…" She bit her lip.

"I think it's a safe bet he knows who—and what—I am," Carch said wryly. The bullet made it plain the assassin was from Galifrax. No doubt a traitor out to kill him before he could recover the Imperial Star and save the king from disaster. "But you don't need to worry—"

He stopped abruptly, all at once realizing what she was doing. Avoiding the real issue, which was going upstairs with him. "Are you *afraid* of me, angel?"

She choked a little, and asked, "Should I be?"

"Devils of Taron, no." But he supposed he didn't blame her. "Tell you what, I'll tend to the floor down here and you can go upstairs first. There are five bedrooms. Take any one you like. They all have baths. Mine is the big one on the right. It has a shower and a Jacuzzi tub." He gave her a sultry smile. "In case your curiosity gets the better of you."

She didn't reply, just whirled and ran up the stairs. Had she even heard what he'd said?

At least she hadn't run for the front door.

He grinned to himself. And he suddenly wondered just how strong her curiosity was about him. She was a science teacher, after all. Surely a little experimentation was in order. Preferably involving the physical compatibility of two alien species.

He really hoped she wasn't afraid of him, just in shock, as she'd said, that her natural curiosity would win out.

Because, although he had every intention of telling her exactly what was going on—for her protection—from now on, he could not let her out of his sight—for his own.

She had seen him. She knew what he was. An alien being. One word from her to the wrong person and he could easily be thrown into a nightmare situation, unable to extract himself. Unable to find the Imperial Star in time to meet his transport home in four days. Unable to save his family from disgrace and probable death.

No. Until he left this planet, he must keep her with him at all times. Either with her consent or, in the worst case, as his captive.

There was no denying, things would be a whole lot easier if her curiosity was greater than her fear.

But how to convince her to trust herself, with any luck her body, and maybe even her life, to a man from outer space?

Chapter 6

Seri blindly hurled herself through the very first door she came to upstairs and smacked it shut behind her. She dropped her suitcase and wrapped her hands over her eyes.

Omigod.

Omigod.

Omigod.

An alien. An extraterrestrial.

An honest-to-God spaceman.

The man downstairs right this minute, the man she had calmly sat next to and eaten lunch with, the man she had—she paled to think of it—*kissed*—was a *creature from another planet!*

Uncontrollable shivers quaked through her body. *This can not be happening.* She swallowed down the terror, desperately trying to calm herself, as she had somehow managed to do while in his presence. She didn't know which part of the situation to deal with first. My God, what the hell was going on here?

Her mind was still reeling from all she'd seen.

She touched shaking fingers to the blood smeared across her dress. So much blood! That anyone could survive being wounded so badly was nothing short of a miracle. But a miracle was exactly what she'd witnessed. How had Carch changed his form like that? She'd read novels about shape-shifters. But to actually see it with her own eyes, to witness it happening! She didn't know whether to be horrified or…fascinated.

Were all aliens able to alter their appearance at will? An awful thought struck her. How many of the people she had met during her lifetime were really from other planets?

She choked out a strangled laugh. *Getting paranoid?* She was really losing it. Show her one man from Plan Nine and she was already imagining a whole slew of alien beings inhabiting Earth.

Calm down, girl!

This was not like her. She had to get hold of herself. She had to start thinking rationally. Logically. Scientifically.

A shower. Fresh clothes. That's what she needed. A return to normalcy—at least outwardly. Then maybe she could analyze the situation. Begin to put back together the pieces of her familiar world. Toss out the insanity that appeared to be overtaking it.

Regain control.

If nothing else, for the sake of her fellow human beings. To find out what this spaceman was doing here. What he wanted. How many more of them were out there…

With decisive movements, Seri marched into the bathroom, stripped out of her ruined clothes, turned the shower faucets to full blast, and stepped through the glass door into the transparent cubicle.

The initial cold-water spray gave her just the jolt she needed to snap her out of the sense of unreality. The solid feel of the tile wall as she leaned her forehead against it lent her strength. Delicious warm water followed the cold, flowing over her, soothing the trembling of her body, soaking her with the optimism of its familiar comfort. She took a deep breath and let it out again.

When you thought about it, she'd been given an amazing gift. The opportunity of a lifetime. Of the century, or even the millennium! She, Serenity June Woodson, was one of the few people ever to meet a real, live alien! It was incredible!

Or…maybe she had just imagined the whole damned thing. Yeah. That was it. Had to be. Space aliens? Get over it.

Just then the bathroom door swung wide and Carch walked in. His astonished gaze landed on her in the shower and he came to an abrupt halt.

Her pulse stalled. The glass cubicle sides were a little fogged up, but one thing was obvious even through the thin layer of steam. He was as naked as she.

Well, almost. He was wearing a tight pair of boxer briefs. But the rest of his body was nude, glorious and glowingly gold in all its alien beauty.

Okay, so maybe she hadn't imagined the whole thing.

He definitely looked real. Maybe too real, she thought as she wiped the fog off a narrow strip of glass in front of her face.

"You're in my shower," he said, peering in at her.

She couldn't tell what his expression meant. His features were so similar to human, similar enough for recognition, yet exotically different. His face was a touch longer than a human's, his crystal-blue eyes a bit wider, and slanted, almost like a Siamese cat's. His features were sharper, and yet the overall effect was softer than a normal male face. A warrior's visage but a lover's mien.

Even under the hot spray of the shower, she shivered at the way he looked at her.

"I'm sorry," she said, quickly shutting off the faucets. Wondering how to cover herself when the nearest towel was at least five feet outside the shower stall, close to where he stood. The steam clinging to the clear walls of the cubicle offered little modesty to begin with, and had already started to condense and run down in long droplets. "I didn't really hear which room…"

Her words trailed off as his gaze slid slowly over her naked body behind the quickly disappearing fog.

She swallowed heavily. He was getting aroused.

Very aroused.

Ho boy.

"Are you sure?" he asked, his thick eyelashes rising. They were golden, too. Like his skin and hair. His whole body was bathed in a golden glow that shimmered around him.

"Wh-what?" she stammered.

"Why are you in my shower?"

"I—"

The steam had dissipated by now and his gaze sought her breasts, perusing them thoroughly. She felt the tips tighten to hard points, pulling at her center in taut, hot threads.

She started to tremble again. This time from a whole different kind of fear. She hugged her arms across her body. She couldn't possibly be *attracted* to the man? Er, spaceman?

His nostrils flared. "I think you knew exactly which room this was. I think you came in here on purpose."

She shook her head. "No. I was confused. Frightened."

Or was he right? Shouldn't she be a lot more alarmed? More worried about her nakedness, about what this alien man intended to do to her? Suddenly, she wasn't so sure. Which confused her even more.

He tilted his elegant head, taking in her protective posture. "Are you still? Frightened and confused?"

"Yes," she said, her voice cracking. Honestly, she was. Terrified.

A hint of that knowing smile slid across his lips. "Would you like me to go, then?"

For several pounding heartbeats they stood in absolute silence except for the knocking of her knees, each taking the measure of the other.

Okay, maybe not so much terrified.

"Well?"

"No," she whispered, barely keeping the panic at bay. Panic…and something else.

Excitement.

Suddenly, she could think of nothing but the searingly sensual kiss they'd shared. How much she'd liked it—kissing him.

And with a blaze of heat, she realized she *wanted* to touch him. Wanted to explore his magnificent body with her own hands. Wanted to learn what a man from another planet felt like. What moved him. What made him cry out. What it felt like to be with him, intimately. And this time it wasn't some weird effect of him touching her.

No. She was a scientist. It was her duty to find out these things.

He took a few steps toward her. "Put your hands on the glass," he ordered softly. "Wide apart. I want to see you."

Her heart thundered. But she hesitated only a moment, then pried her hands loose from her body and placed them against the slick, wet surface, palms out. Carch moved to the door, but instead of opening it, he reached up to match his hands to hers on the other side of the transparent barrier.

Instantly, she felt that low thrum of…energy…hum between their hands, even through the glass. It felt like the buzz of a trapped honey bee—restless, electric, with an edge of danger, an unmistakable warning of its painful sting, and yet a siren tease for its sweet, sweet honey.

"How do you do that?" she whispered, forgetting all about her nakedness and her embarrassment.

He just smiled. And snicked open the door. With a quailing heart, she watched him enter, his muscles rippling with contained strength, his cat eyes glittering with unconcealed anticipation.

Her breath faltered, along with her courage. He was so close. *Too close.* He was so…exotic. *So different. Not human.* Instinctively, she stepped backward, away from him. Her bare back hit cool, solid tile.

He reached out, gently stroking her cheek with his finger-tips. His touch tingled as always, but stronger this time. It sent a quiver deep down into her body, straight to her aching center. She sucked in a gulp of air, squeezed her eyes shut, waiting with a thrill of fear for that warm roll of his presence through her mind that always followed his touch.

He closed the scant distance between them, raised his other hand to her face and traced her features with his long, tapered fingers. She shook uncontrollably.

"You want me," he murmured softly, soothingly. "But I can feel your terror of my otherness. I'll shift back to my human shape, so my appearance is not so upsetting."

"No!" she said in a sudden rush, her eyes opening. She licked her dry lips. "It's true. I'm terrified. But I want to see you as you really are, to know your true form."

He regarded her for a long moment, a moment during which she felt the warmth of his admiration wash through her physically as though an affirming wave. "Brave girl," he murmured, and kissed her. With his beautiful bronze lips.

He tasted the same as he had before. Musty with a dusting of delicious exotic spice. His tongue felt the same, too. Long. Supple. Breathtakingly talented. It was like he knew exactly what she craved, and gave it to her just when she wanted it most. His kiss left her lightheaded, dizzy with the want for more of him.

"How do you do that?" she asked again in an awe-filled whisper.

He chuckled softly. "What? Kiss? Pretty much the same way Earth men do."

"No, you don't." No one had ever kissed her like that before. So thoroughly. So…amazingly. "Not even close. And when you touch me, that's different, too. It's like you reach inside me. I can actually feel you there, inside me."

He nodded, tracing his fingers around her throat to the back of her neck. "I am an empath. When I touch you, my mind can enter yours and I can sense your emotions, I feel what you feel."

She stared up at him, stunned. She didn't think she liked that. "So I can have no secrets from you?" *No control.*

After an infinitesimal pause, he said, "None that I don't allow you." His other hand slid around her waist, pulling her close. "But don't worry, I shall confine myself to your sexual feelings for now."

Her face heated at his almost casual attitude toward what they were doing. Which, somewhere along the line, she must have consented to, if only by not slamming the shower door on him. By letting him touch her. Yes, she had consented, and more. She'd wanted this. Wanted *him.*

What had become of her usual modesty, her standard reserve against all things sexual? Had she lost it because she was treating this encounter as a purely scientific experiment?

She didn't have a chance to think about that because he kissed her again, and when he kissed her she couldn't think at all, she could just stand there helplessly clinging to him and hope she'd survive the blinding pleasure.

He pressed his body to hers so that they touched all the way from their lips to their toes. Everywhere their skin met, she felt as though she were melting into him. It was as if she was slowly seeping into the warm, golden, liquid glow of Carch Sunstryker. He was so tall and strong, and his body felt so good against hers, so hard and muscular under the glowing layer of gold. It felt so wonderful to have to stretch on her tiptoes to wrap her arms around his neck. And it was pure heaven when his amazing mouth joined with hers.

His tongue knew just what to do, how to tease hers, just how to seduce her into responding, just how to stir her excitement to a fever pitch.

All too soon the kiss ended. He lifted his head and gazed down at her with a very masculine curve to his lips. *Carch's lips.* He'd shifted his face back to its human form.

"You kept thinking of me as an alien," he said when he saw her surprise. "At the moment, I only want you to think of me as an ordinary man."

Suddenly, he frowned. "Damn. I'm sorry." His hand brushed softly at her chest and shoulder. "I've gotten blood on you. I should have washed before touching you like that."

He reached behind her and turned on the faucet again, adjusting it so the warm water sprayed over both of them.

"I didn't even see the blood," she admitted. It had been overshadowed by the thick luminescence of his skin.

The force of the shower spray rinsed the red off in rivulets until most of it was gone. She touched her fingers to the flawless flesh above his heart where he'd been shot. "There's no trace of the wound."

He smiled. "One of the advantages of being a shapeshifter."

"You were lucky."

"Very lucky," he agreed, "because I had you to help. Any more blood loss and I would have blacked out. I couldn't have completed the shift. I owe you my life, angel."

She was about to ask him why he called her angel, but he leaned down and kissed her tenderly. Ah, well, she was getting used to the nickname. In fact, she was starting to like it. Almost as much as she liked his kisses.

He pulled away again. "You are far too distracting. I should wash before this goes any further."

The implication of what would come next was plain. Her skin flushed hot. But strangely, she only felt more excited. More aroused. She picked up the bottle of shower gel. "Let me," she murmured. Then halted when she saw he was still wearing his boxer briefs. Her eyes darted to his.

He looked amused. "Think you're ready to see all of me?"

She swallowed. "I've seen a man naked before."

He tipped up her chin with a finger. "There are…differences."

"Such as?"

He pursed his sculpted lips, drinking in her expression as though soaking up the heat and flame in her cheeks. Then gave his golden head a shake. "No. I don't believe my little scientist is quite ready for that. I should shift."

"But—"

"At least down there. I am vain enough to want you thinking of the man who is pleasuring you, not the equipment."

She felt a spurt of frustration. "Why not both?"

A rumbling chuckle vibrated against her. "You must be patient. You won't be disappointed even now. I promise you." He gave her a smile that told her he intended to make good on that promise in every way possible. "Would you like to see what I have for you?"

She clutched the bottle of shower gel tight in her fingers. And nodded.

His smile widened, and he reached for his boxers.

Chapter 7

Carch always thought of each new woman he coupled with as a fresh, blank canvas to be lovingly body-painted in a unique style all her own. He rather liked the image of himself as the consummate artist, using all the tools at his disposal to render an erotic masterpiece for her, one she would dream of and sigh over for the rest of her life.

But this time, it wasn't turning out quite that way. This time, Seri was doing all the painting, and *he* was doing all the sighing.

Make that groaning.

There was definitely something askew with this picture. But for the moment he was content—all right, helpless—to let it unfold just as it was.

Seri had anointed him with shower gel and was using her hands to coax it into a voluminous lather as she explored his body. Every inch of it. The feeling was exquisite. Better than exquisite. It was orgasmic.

On his part, anyway.

For hers, he still detected a certain distance in her feelings, a lingering notion of objective experimentation. It was maddening that he should be hot enough to blast off and she so damned reserved.

"I love your skin," she murmured in a worshipful voice, somewhat mollifying him. "So smooth."

At least she was enjoying the study. He'd meant to shift his form completely, to be a familiar human male for her for their first time as lovers. That would have taken care of her annoying detachment.

But she'd protested. "I want to know what the real you feels like. Some of you, anyway," she'd added pointedly.

She'd still been a little miffed that he didn't think she was ready for the whole package. But she wasn't. He'd felt her innocence and inexperience lurking under all that objective bravado.

At least he thought he had. But her hands were telling a different story. Maybe she was a quick study. The whole scientist thing. Stimulus and response. An easy concept. Which she was using to its full potential.

Damn, she was amazing.

"I'm glad I please you," he managed. "Speaking of which, why don't I— Nhhhh…" His attempt to reverse their roles faded into an inarticulate moan as her fingers skimmed the place he most wanted her to touch. "Nhhhh…"

"And I love how your skin glows with that thick, golden light. Look how it swirls around my hands as they move over you."

"It's called glamour," he croaked. And the more aroused he became, the brighter it glowed.

She was amusing herself—and driving him crazy—by blending the sudsy foam and his glamour into flowing patterns that teased both their limbs with a low tickle of energy. He was glowing pretty damn brightly.

Nobody had ever done anything remotely like this to him before. On Galifrax everyone had glamour, and it was seldom used to erotic purposes, save by courtesans in brushes of mild flirtation, and priests who specialized in esoteric tantric sex. He wondered why. The stimulation was subtle, but in combination with fingers and bubbles, incredibly arousing.

She swirled a handful of glittering lather around his rampant sex and he forgot to breathe. She tipped her head and lightly touched him.

The air exploded from his lungs as he grabbed for her wrists, and for dominion. "Enough," he gritted out, piqued with her damn experimentation. "I believe I'm more than clean. It's my turn now."

He held her captured wrists behind her back and moved with her under the still-hot spray to rinse the foaming gel from their bodies. And took her mouth in a bruising kiss.

He was ravenous for her.

He was done with science. Done with teasing. Done with foreplay.

He wanted the real thing.

Shutting off the water he swept her up into his arms. Her eyes widened and he could feel the swift hammer of her heartbeat as he carried her from the bathroom to his bed.

"What are you doing?" she asked anxiously.

"Take a wild guess."

"But I thought—"

"Thought what? To string me along as your complacent lab rat without having to pay the price? I'm afraid not, my love." He dropped her onto the bed and climbed on top of her, wedging his knee between her legs to part them. "That was a real man you were touching in there, not a specimen under a microscope. I tolerated your probing quite well, I thought. Now. How well shall you tolerate mine?"

"Carch, wait."

"What?" he ground out.

"Will I get pregnant?"

He stopped for a quick moment to consider. The odds were astronomical against it. "No," he told her.

Water dripped from his long hair down the sides of her crimson cheeks. Her wide green eyes looked huge in her ivory-pale face, framed by her slick, reddish locks. Her soft, rosy lips parted, admitting quick, shallow breaths. Her damp skin was beaded with drops of water and goose flesh, her breasts pert, tight and heaving.

She didn't make a sound, but her legs quivered, then deliberately fell apart, letting him slide between them.

He didn't wait. He grasped her thighs, pulled them wide and plunged into her.

They both cried out.

Moradth, she was tight as a glove and felt better than anything he'd ever experienced.

He halted, grinding his jaw, and gathered her in his arms. "Are you all right?" he asked.

"Yes." But her voice was thready.

"No pain? I can make myself smaller."

"No. You're perfect." She adjusted her body under him, lifted her knees, and he slid in deeper.

They both moaned softly.

He could feel her pleasure. Could feel her amazement. And her vague disbelief and slight distress over how much pleasure she did feel with his alien sex buried deep within her. Then there was confusion and denial, and suddenly her terror returned in a rush.

"Shhh," he crooned in her ear as she squirmed under him,

and he cradled her securely in his embrace. "It's all right to let yourself feel the pleasure. No need to be frightened. It's just an ordinary mating."

Holding her tighter, he pulled himself nearly out of her, then thrust back in. For a moment they were both breathless from the sensation. He licked at her mouth, which had parted on another moan.

"Good?" he soothed, and she gave an almost reluctant nod.

With his gentle encouragement he felt her muscles uncoil, just a little, and her inner chaos of sleeping with a man not human abated somewhat.

"You see? Nothing but pleasure."

Her arms tightened around his neck. "Yes," she murmured. "I see."

But there was still some small, hidden fear in the back of her mind, so veiled he couldn't get to it.

"Angel," he whispered. "Stay with me and I'll make you forget everything but the pleasure. I promise."

She gazed up at him, her face open, vulnerable. Her eyes wanting so much to trust him. He didn't know what to do except kiss her. Kiss away the doubt. Kiss away that fear lurking just below the surface of her courage, kiss away her damned reserve.

He kissed her long and hard. Until she melted beneath him and her body became warm putty that he could form and reform to his whim, which he did, using his fingers and his hands, his tongue and lips and his thick, demanding sex.

A long, long while later, when he was finished with her, he saw with satisfaction that the fear was gone. There was only him in her eyes. Only him in her mind. Only him for her body. Only him.

He lay with his limbs stretched out over hers, sated, the glow of his glamour dimmed with repletion, and he smiled.

An odd sort of possessiveness swept through him as he gazed down at her languid form. Despite her fears, she'd given herself more thoroughly in their lovemaking than any other woman ever had. He had striven hard to please her, and she had responded to his efforts so sweetly and completely that he in turn had been pleasured by her tenfold.

Was this what the men in his family saw in Earth women? This incredible generosity?

His objective had been to make her an ally in his quest. To make her remain with him until his mission was finished. But he was the one who didn't want to leave the bed. Didn't want to leave her.

She had won him over without even trying.

Her eyes were closed, so with a wince he allowed his body to complete the short transformation to full human form. He wanted no reminders of his otherness to intrude on the moment when she looked at him for the first time in the new light of their being lovers. As a human, that relationship would mean something to her. It would bond her to him even further.

And to be honest, if she opened her eyes and still looked at him as though he was some kind of experiment, he would—

He clamped his jaw. The vehemence of the anger that swept through him at the thought shocked him. Where had it come from? Why did it matter so much that she think of him as just a man, not as an alien male? That distinction had never bothered him before in his travels through the galaxies.

Disturbed, he rolled off her and onto his back on the mattress beside her. Her eyes cracked open and she glanced over at him. Her tongue kept silent but her eyes questioned.

He forced a smile, and said, "On some planets we'd be married now."

She froze for a nanosecond, then returned his bland smile. "Lucky for you we're on Earth, then."

"Is it?" He raised a brow, turning to her. For some reason her new sangfroid over what they'd just done ticked him off royally. What had happened to bonding? Or better yet, starstruck worship? That hadn't been unheard of in his past.

"Aren't you even a little worried," he asked in even tones, "that by joining your flesh with mine you have committed yourself to some unwanted or even unholy alien alliance?"

She gazed at him for a second, then said, "No."

More irritation swept through him. "What makes you so certain?"

"You said it was an ordinary mating. Besides, you're not the kind of man who, it strikes me, would allow himself to be saddled with anything he didn't want, especially a woman."

His reaction was swift and powerful. "Who says I don't want you?" He grasped her jaw in his palm. "I believe I just proved how much I do want you. And maybe now that I've had a taste of your gifts I want you even more. Maybe enough to shatter that objective certainty of yours."

Her eyes flared as his body quickened to prove his point. But that small flare was her only indication of apprehension...outwardly. On the inside, however, his touch let him read the sudden alarm filling her mind. Oh, she was afraid all right. As well she should be. He was a royal prince of Galifrax, and could have anything—and anyone—he wanted.

He forced a calming breath.

Strangely, he sensed it was not the prospect of being abducted to another planet by him that worried her. It was something else. Something to do with Carch's grandfather. And with her own father. A feeling of...abandonment?

She wrenched away, turned her face from him. "Stop it!" she said. "I can feel you in my mind, and it's not fair."

He shook himself free of the unpleasant emotion. No

wonder she'd retreated behind her protective facade of cold, hard facts. He reached out to reassure her. But stopped himself.

Because abandoning her was exactly what he intended to do. After indulging in the pleasures of her body while they tracked down the Imperial Star, he would rocket away back to Galifrax with the necklace in tow. But not with her.

Ouch.

"I'm sorry," he said. Truthfully, the last thing he wanted was to hurt her. But his mission was far more important than her fragile human feelings. He would do anything to recover the Imperial Star and save his family. She had to understand that.

Except…

Except she didn't know.

He sat up in bed and dragged his fingers through his hair. She watched him warily.

Should he tell her everything?

Could he trust her with the truth?

She looked so beautiful lying there in his bed amidst the rumpled sheets and disheveled pillows, her mussed hair spread out like flames against the white of the sheets. Her body was perfect, her breasts full and ripe, her limbs long and trim. The musky scent of their lovemaking hovered in the air, stirring his arousal with the memories they'd so recently made together. She had been magnificent. A wonderful bed partner.

The thought of leaving her behind sent another unexpected wave of possessiveness crashing through his body.

He couldn't help himself. He had to have her again.

In a single movement he was on top of her and spreading her legs with his knees. And then he was inside her, scything himself deep, deep into her accepting body. She made a noise, part pleasure, part something that may have been desperation. He covered her mouth with his and dug his fingers into the flesh of her thighs, gripping and plunging into her over and over.

She clung to him, molding the shape of his biceps with her palms, arching into him so her breasts rubbed the crisp smattering of hair that covered his chest, raking her nails over the expanse of his human-broad back. All the while crying out at his thrusts, meeting his hips with her own in a strong, primitive rhythm. The pitch of her cries rose, more and more sublime, and more and more desperate, until her body convulsed around him.

He didn't let up. Not until he'd ridden her to the crest again and her body trembled limply under him, her flesh quivering, and she gazed up at him in total, blissful submission. Only then did he allow himself to let loose the bonds of his own pleasure.

Feeling the fierce bite of climax fast approach, he gave three more powerful thrusts. And the irrational thought that had ridden his consciousness as he had ridden her burst free. As he shook with his final pleasure, he punctuated each explosion of orgasm with a low growl in her ear.

"You. Are. Mine."

Chapter 8

Descending back to Earth after that breathtaking statement, Seri told herself there was no need to panic. Carch didn't mean it literally. "You are mine" was just one of those things a man said in the heat of climax to the woman who happened to be under him.

Her lover had a fierce look about him as he collapsed panting onto her, burying his face in the pillow. He had been ferocious. Especially that last time. She felt thoroughly taken. Ravaged. If he'd been human, she might be worried about his intensity.

But he wasn't human.

Should she panic anyway? What did it mean in his culture to claim a woman so completely?

Her breath was coming in great gulps, as was his, their bodies entwined in a slick, hot tangle of limbs. He had taken what he wanted, at times roughly, at times gently. But never had he given her anything but pleasure. Or any indication that this was anything more than what he claimed it to be. Ordinary sex.

Okay, maybe ordinary for him. For her, extraordinary.

But still, just sex. No reason to panic.

Besides, panic took energy. And she didn't have a single joule left in her body. Carch had drained her completely.

She did manage a smile at that image. Not exactly how the UFO flicks depicted aliens draining humans of their life force. Except perhaps those of the It-Came-*in*-Outer-Space variety.

"Are you giggling?" A muffled, half-insulted rumble sounded from deep in the pillow next to her ear.

"From pleasure," she assured him, her breath and pulse finally slowing. She found she enjoyed the weight and movement of his large body on hers as he wound down, too. "Pure, amazing pleasure."

He lifted his head and smiled down at her. "Ah. Good."

He was still cradled between her thighs, still reposing inside her. She rubbed her hands slowly over his back, feeling the full expanse of his shoulders and the steely strength of his muscular arms. "You shifted all the way," she murmured.

Rationally, she should be more afraid of him in his alien form, but for some reason this all-human body made her shiver more. It was so big, so powerful, so...very male.

"We should probably get up," he said, trailing a finger along her cheek. "Try to get in one or two more pawn shops before they close."

She gave a guilty start. The hunt for Aunt Tildy's necklace! In the heat of their passion, she'd completely forgotten about it. They must have been in bed for a couple of hours, but a glance at the window told her the sun was still a ways from setting.

"Good idea," she said, struggling not to let an illogical disappointment take hold.

What's wrong with me?

She could definitely use some distance from Carch to regain her usual sensible perspective. She had expected sex. What she'd gotten was so much more that it had knocked her totally off balance. But with his magnificent body lying on top of hers, it was impossible to think.

She waited for him to roll off her. He didn't.

"Angel, there's something I need to tell you."

Something in his tone, the subtle warning in it, made her come to attention. Her pulse quickened. And not necessarily in a good way. Their position was intimate, but suddenly a wary stranger was looking down at her. A wary stranger who could easily control her every move from where he lay atop her.

"Okay," she said, carefully neutral, but her heart pounding.

"I want you to know about the necklace," he said. "I want you to know what's at stake if we don't find it."

Her heart froze for a second, then sank. The implication of his words was clear. Damn it! He *was* after her aunt's necklace.

She'd been right all along.

What a fool she'd been to trust him!

He must have sensed her acute disappointment for he took hold of her upper arms. "It's nothing that will affect Tildy, I swear. Please, just hear me out."

Selfishly, it wasn't Aunt Tildy she was thinking about.

"Fine," she said. "As soon as you let me up."

After a heartbeat's hesitation he put his hand to her cheek and kissed her. "Thank you, angel," he whispered, "for a wonderful mating."

She blinked. Wow. The Galifracian take on romantic?

Nothing like a double-slap of cold, hard reality to set a girl straight.

"You're welcome," she said politely. This time she didn't wait for him to move, she gave him a firm push to roll him off. Then she went straight for her suitcase, still sitting by the door where she had dropped it when she'd rushed in after learning he came from another planet.

Which now seemed like a hundred years ago.

And it also seemed—big shocker—there wasn't such a huge difference between males, regardless of which planet they came from. Men had their own agendas. They'd use you, then leave you. It's what men did. That was the lesson she'd learned early on from her father. And no man since had done anything to convince her otherwise. Not even one who wasn't human.

Comforting, in a perverted sort of way.

Time to take back control.

"Talk," she said as she started to dress.

He didn't speak right away, but sat in bed, leaning against the headboard with his hands stacked behind his head, watching her put on her clothes.

"What's wrong?" he finally asked.

"Nothing."

"You're angry."

"You think?"

She reined in her galloping disillusionment. How was it possible to go from fear to elation to disappointment so quickly? She should have known better than to trust anything that happened in bed. She had only herself to blame for forgetting. She didn't *do* men, and this was exactly why.

"I'm angry with myself, not you."

"Why?"

She buttoned the top button of her blouse. "I have trouble curbing my curiosity, and also trusting my own instincts. I really need to work on that. But instincts have never been my forte."

He frowned. "What's that supposed to mean?"

She couldn't look at him because he was still naked—precisely what had gotten her into trouble in the first place.

Sadly irrational, but true. Where was her legendary control when she needed it?

"It means that sleeping with you was such a bad idea in so many ways I can't believe I did it. I should have been able to stop myself."

His frown deepened. "You're sorry we had sex? I thought I pleased you."

"You did, Carch. It's not that. It's—" She shook her head and slid on her skirt. Why bother? A man would not understand. This was a woman thing. "Never mind. What is it you have to tell me? And please, get dressed."

He didn't look happy, but didn't push it, thank God. He got up and went to the dresser.

She couldn't see his face, but his voice sounded low and clear as he dug through a drawer. "My grandfather, Derrik Sunstryker, is king of Galifrax. It is a position that is part hereditary and part elected, the king being chosen by and from among all Fracian noble families. The title is for life. Unless something happens to cause the nobles to call his honor into question."

"Derrik," she mused, watching him pull on a pair of well-fitting jeans. "The man Aunt Tildy talks about. I thought he was a prince."

"He was at the time he met her."

Reluctantly she asked, "So it's true, everything she says about him?"

"Yes," Carch said. "He visited Earth as a young man and they met."

She sat down on the edge of the bed. "Are there a lot of you Galifracians here on Earth?"

He slanted her an amused smile. "No. We usually send a scientific expedition to drop by every fifty years or so, to see what you humans are up to. But when the ship leaves, everyone is on it. It's one of our stricter laws."

"No influencing the primitives?"

He chuckled humorlessly. "Something like that. But there are no laws against others coming to our planet. So when my grandfather and Tildy fell in love, he asked her to come back with him."

She tried to imagine what it must have been like for her aunt to fall in love with an alien prince. Unfortunately, it was not such a stretch.

She cleared her throat. "As I recall the story, he was married at the time. With a child, too."

Carch nodded somberly. "Yes. My father. But you have to understand. On my planet, couples rarely stay together for life. Most don't even bother to marry. Three or four, even five partners are quite common over a lifetime. It is expected."

Good grief. Sounded like a nightmare to her. "No wonder Aunt Tildy said no."

He sent her a wry look. "Spoken like a true Earthling. There are exceptions, Seri. But as you know, that wasn't why she turned him down."

"It was because of my mother."

Seri could hear the admiration in Carch's voice when he said, "Yes. Tildy is a very loyal woman. She wouldn't leave her dying sister. Not even for the love of a nobleman who could give her everything her heart desired and more."

"Except her sister's life."

"Except that," Carch agreed quietly.

Seri looked down at her hands, twining in her lap. "My mother would surely have died if Tildy hadn't stayed to nurse her through the hepatitis. They had very little money and couldn't afford to send her to a sanatorium."

"If she'd died, you would never have been born."

"True enough," Seri said somberly. She looked up to find him standing in front of her. "My parents didn't meet until eight years later, a long time after she recovered."

Carch's fingers brushed a stray lock of hair from her forehead. "Bad luck for Derrik. Good luck for me."

He had a peculiar look on his face, which smoothed out when their eyes met again.

"Don't be so sure," she murmured.

"Anyway, when my grandfather was about to leave, he tried one last time to get Tildy to come with him. She held out stubbornly, even though it was breaking both their hearts." Carch blew out a breath. "And that's when my grandfather did the unthinkable."

Seri gazed at him expectantly. That damned curiosity again. "He gave her the necklace?"

"With a promise to come back for her—and the necklace—when the time was right."

Yeah, sure he would. "So why didn't he ever come back?"

"Shortly after his return he was elected king. The king is not allowed off-planet, for any reason."

Ah. Well, at least he had a good excuse.

"The thing is," Carch continued, "he claims he also left it with her for safekeeping. That he'd learned his rival for the kingship had hatched a plot to use it against him, to seize power."

"Under the circumstances, that makes more sense."

Carch looked grim. "No, it doesn't. Regardless of his suspicions, he must have been insane. If he failed to return for it, he knew what the consequences could be. Would most likely be. But apparently falling in love turns one's brains to mush."

Ignoring his cynical remark about love, Seri asked, "What consequences? And why? Because it's some alien material that we aren't familiar with on Earth? That influencing-the-primitives thing?"

"Actually, no. The necklace is made of gold and gems fairly similar to those native to this planet. Although it is definitely against our laws to leave behind any kind of evidence of our existence."

"Why, then?"

Carch rubbed his temple in agitation. "Because it is a very special necklace, with very unique powers. It's part of a set used by the royal priesthood for a particular ceremony that is held every fifty-two years. My family has been its caretaker for over a millennium. If it is discovered that the Imperial Star is missing, we will be blamed."

Seri had her first tingle of true foreboding. Whatever explanation she had thought he'd give for being after her aunt's necklace, this wasn't even close. Perhaps she'd misjudged him, after all. "What will happen?"

"The family will be charged with treason."

Shock went through her. "*Treason?* But that's—"

"It's a sacred relic. Believe me, our enemies will make much of its loss. My grandfather will certainly be dethroned and executed, and—"

"*Executed!* My God, Carch—"

"And chances are, the rest of us will be, too."

Us?

She dropped her jaw in mute horror, unable to grasp the reality of what he was saying.

He nodded at her unspoken question. "Yes, me included."

"But that's— That's—" How could he stand there so calmly and discuss his own execution? His execution over a piece of *jewelry!* It was outrageous! Good lord, no wonder he was so anxious to get it back.

"That's why my grandfather sent me to retrieve it. And why our enemies have obviously sent someone to stop me."

Her gaze dropped to his chest. "The shooting."

She frowned, appalled. "But…why don't your grandfaer's enemies simply tell everyone the necklace is gone? Vouldn't that have been easier?"

"They don't dare. They can't have been certain it was issing, not until one of them followed me here and actually w it around Tildy's neck. If they'd accused the king and been rong, it would have been *them* accused of treason."

"I guess that makes sense."

"Whoever it is knows that if I find the necklace and have back on Galifrax before the end of next month, no one will e the wiser. They will have lost their best and possibly last ance to seize power."

The breath she'd been taking burst from her lungs. "What? ack on Galifrax by next month? How far— How long does take to get there?"

He took her hands and smiled. "Ever my practical angel. he ship takes just over a month to reach our galaxy. Then other few days to Galifrax."

Goose bumps swept down her arms. It could be a lot orse. "So you have four weeks to find the necklace. You ould be able to—"

"Not exactly," he interrupted.

She gazed up at him, not liking his expression. "Why?"

"My transport home will be here in four days. The crew nows nothing about my real mission. They think it's a routine ientific expedition, so they'll expect to pick me up and take ff immediately. I must have the necklace by then."

Oh, God. "Four days?"

"Actually, three and a half."

She didn't give herself a chance to think, just jumped up d started for the door, grabbing her purse on the way. "Then ere's no time to lose."

His footfalls sounded just behind her on the stairs. "You're ill willing to help me?"

"Of course I'll help you. It'll break Aunt Tildy's heart t give up the necklace, but she'll understand."

"Actually, I'm having a duplicate made for her. That's wh I didn't ask for it back sooner. I could kill myself for not takin possession of it right away, for not keeping it safe."

She cringed as they reached the front foyer and sh recalled vividly what had happened there earlier. "Appar ently someone else feels the same way. The part abou killing you, I mean." She wrapped her arms around hersel nervously, glancing at the pristine floor that had so recentl been covered in Carch's blood. "Are you sure it's safe fo you to go out?"

"There's an alternative?"

"I could—"

He shook his head. "I am a prince. I fight my own battles He took hold of her hands. "And I'd never forgive myself anything happened to you."

"It's not me they're after, Carch."

"No. It's power they're after. A king's power. And they'll us any means at their disposal to get it. Hurting you would be last resort, but I'm afraid they might do it if it helps their cause

She shuddered at the blatant worry in his words. An suddenly was more terrified than she'd ever been in her life

What in the world have I got myself mixed up in?

This morning she had just been a plain, ordinary hig school science teacher living a plain, ordinary, boring life Now she was involved in intergalactic intrigue, royal powe plays, treason and assassinations.

Not to mention sleeping with a man from another planet

She put her hand over her mouth to stifle the small soun of utter disbelief that wanted to come out. Was she goin nuts? Or was this all real?

"They won't get the chance to hurt you, angel," Carch sai

obviously misinterpreting the source of her distress. He folded her in his embrace. "I'll protect you with my life. I swear."

It felt so good being sheltered in his strong arms that she swallowed her hitched breath and refrained from pointing out that it was hard to protect someone if you were dead.

Of course, if he were dead, the traitors would have already won. Carch wouldn't let that happen.

Hell, *she* wouldn't let that happen.

"I'll protect you, too," she whispered, holding him tight instead of running as far and as fast as she could from this crazy situation. Especially from him. Which was just what she would do if she had even half a brain.

He smiled wistfully down at her. "I should lock you in my bedroom and throw away the key, to keep you safe," he said. "And I would, if I didn't need your help. Three and a half days is not a very long time."

"Nah," she said, drawing herself up confidently. "Three and a half days will be plenty." She looked up into his concerned face. "After all," she said, "how hard can it be to find one measly necklace?"

Chapter 9

God, she was amazing.

If the situation weren't so serious, Carch would have swept his sweet Seri up into his arms and kissed her silly.

Damn, no man had ever been so loyal and courageous in Carch's aid before, let alone a woman—other than his non-Galifracian mother, of course. Fracian women were far more apt to blend into the woodwork and disappear at the least sign of trouble than to offer to help a man. He had always thought this right and proper. Women had women's concerns and men had men's, and seldom did the two converge. Except in bed. That was the way it was, and had always been, on Galifrax.

But not on Earth.

Carch had spent the past weeks recognizing his mother's irritatingly independent and frustratingly contrary personality in most of the other Earth women he met. It had bugged him to no end.

But now he was starting to see the error of his judgment.

"We have plenty of time to find the necklace," Seri said with conviction. "If we go about our search efficiently and methodically."

"Let's hope you're right." He headed for the front door. "The good news is, the fact that I was shot at means my enemy must not have the necklace either."

"Or he'd be long gone, hightailing it back to Galifrax," Seri agreed.

"Or at least in hiding, if he came on the same ship as me."

"Which in turn begs the original question."

"And that is…?"

She gave him a considering look. "If your enemy didn't take the necklace, who did?"

After fetching his Mercedes, Carch and Seri discussed various possibilities while they were driving around to the three pawnshops they wanted to squeeze in before closing time. But they kept going around in theoretical circles.

"I still vote for your pals Alan and David from the Thin Man Art Deco Gallery," Carch said, squinting at the addresses along the street, searching for the first pawnshop. He doubted locating the missing necklace would be as easy as walking across the courtyard, but one could always hope. Although, judging by the luck—or lack of it—they'd had at the pawn shops, they were probably in for a long haul.

"Aunt Tildy seems convinced it was Madam Clarissa," Seri countered.

Either way was fine with him. As long as he got the necklace quickly. "Then I suggest their two establishments should be the first places we investigate."

Seri turned to him. "Investigate how?"

How did she think? "Break in, of course. Take a look around."

Her mouth gaped. "Break in? As in...*break in?*"

He grinned. "What's a little B and E among friends?"

Her eyes squeezed shut as she slumped down in the soft leather passenger seat of the Mercedes, mumbling about intergalactic something-or-other and the hoosegow.

Well, what did she expect him to do, knock on the door and politely ask if they'd stolen it?

After striking out at the first two pawnshops, they continued their discussion.

"It's only been a day since the necklace disappeared," he reasoned. "I'll bet it's just lying around waiting for whoever stole it to decide what to do with the thing. If they know Tildy, they'll also know she reported its theft to the police. They have to be afraid of being caught and arrested if they try to fence it."

"So you think we should just break in and steal it back?"

"What would you suggest?"

She blinked. "Use your powers."

"Excuse me?"

"You could read their minds. Our suspects. If they're guilty you'll know it, and *then* we can break in and steal it back."

It sounded logical, but there were just a couple of slight catches. "Angel, I have to confess, I exaggerated a bit when we talked about this before."

"Oh?"

"I'm not as skilled at the mind-reading thing as I might have led you to believe."

"But...I've felt you there, inside my head. I know you can do it."

"And it scared you. So you didn't hide your emotions as easily as you could have."

"Are you saying I can shield my thoughts from you if I try?" She looked stunned, but not unpleasantly so.

He sighed. "I really can't read specific thoughts. Only emotions. And yes, you could shield them if you chose to. A thief will not be as open as you are. It's likely they would just naturally shield the feelings that could give them away."

"But they might not."

"True. The thing is, you always know when I'm probing around inside your head. So would they. They'll know what I'm doing. What if they start speculating on my unusual ability to get inside a person's head? Speculating to the media, for instance? Do you have any idea what will happen to me if word gets out I'm from another planet?"

She looked doubtful. "You'll make the front page of the *Enquirer?* Get real, spaceman. No one will believe it."

"You do."

She squirmed in her seat. "Only because I saw you shape-shift. Hard to ignore that kind of evidence."

"Not everyone is as skeptical as you are. Those tabloids are just looking for a sensational story. And your government isn't as oblivious as it sometimes appears. The military would be all over it. All over *me*." He shook his head. "No, I can't take the chance. I have enough on my plate without worrying about men in black coming after me."

"Men in black?" She rolled her eyes. "A spaceman with a warped sense of humor. Just what I need."

Yeah, well, he might be treating it lightly, but it would definitely be no laughing matter if he were caught. He'd seen firsthand during his space travels what could happen if he were captured by the authorities of a different planet. The sight was not a pretty one.

Not to mention that his being captured would certainly doom his family on Galifrax.

They got back into the car after having no luck with the third and final pawnshop on today's list. He glanced at the clock on the dashboard. "Guess we'd better head back to Tildy's. It's getting late."

He parked close to the Second Sun Crystal and Tarot Salon, where Tildy had invited them for supper at her apartment, and they walked through the shadows of the cool courtyard. He smiled when Seri gave the doorbells a scowl, trying to decide which one to push. She finally decided on the fourth one, the one that said, Press me if revenge or protection is your greatest wish.

"The bells don't really do anything, you know," he said with amusement, idly contemplating whether she was going for the revenge or the protection part.

"Oh, shut up," she muttered, flinging the door open when she realized it wasn't locked. He just laughed.

"Well, well, well. If it isn't Serenity June."

The greeting halted Seri's progress, and she turned toward the scratchy voice echoing through the courtyard. A dark-haired, middle-aged woman stood on the front step of the Palmistry Shoppe watching them. A couple of cats rubbed at her ankles.

"Hello, Madam Clarissa. How's business?" Seri greeted her with a neutral voice.

"Better lately," the woman said with a smug smile. "Didn't take you long to snare that one," she cackled, pointing to Carch.

Talk about rude. He casually slung his arm around Seri and said, "More like the other way around, Clarissa."

"Did that necklace ever turn up that Tildy was asking about yesterday?" the obnoxious woman asked.

"Not yet," Seri said with remarkable restraint. "But don't worry. It will soon."

He didn't care for the gleeful way Madam Clarissa smiled when she disappeared back through her door without another word. Hmm. Maybe Tildy was right about the old bat.

"Looney Tune," Seri muttered under her breath, going into the Second Sun.

"Oh, there you are, my dears!" Tildy exclaimed excitedly when she spotted them. "Did you find it?"

Carch hated to disappoint her. She looked so crestfallen when he told her they hadn't. "We're going to pursue some other leads later tonight. I'm hopeful we'll find the necklace soon."

She sighed as she locked up and preceded them up the stairs. "I certainly hope so. Since it went missing, my tarot readings have been awful." She shook her head bleakly. "It's as though all my psychic abilities have flown away. I look at the cards and my mind is a complete blank."

Carch felt a deep pang of guilt. Tildy had no idea the Imperial Star was the reason for her psychic skills. Without the Imperial Star's special power around her neck, her ability to read people would be considerably diminished, if not eliminated altogether, depending on her latent native talent, which most humans were unable to tap into.

"This is all Madam Clarissa's doing," she said crossly. "I *told* you she was trying to distract me."

Seri went to her aunt and gave her a heartfelt hug. "Don't you worry. It'll all come back to you." She gave him an encouraging look over Tildy's shoulder.

Obviously she wanted him to tell her aunt everything. He had really hoped to avoid that whole conversation by presenting her with the substitute necklace he was having made and pretending it was the real thing. Tildy wouldn't know the difference. And Carch wouldn't have to go into the whole sordid treason-and-execution business, which was sure to upset the old gal. She still had feelings for his grandfather, he could tell.

He decided to stall. "What smells so good?" he asked brightly, knowing that cooking was Tildy's second love after tarot reading, and talking about it would cheer her up. "I hope you haven't gone to too much trouble with dinner."

As it turned out, she had. It was a veritable feast of Charleston delights. Fresh-caught shrimp and savory grits, spicy red rice, a tangy salad and crisp, sweet, just-picked corn. They ate the meal around an old oak table in the cozy kitchen, with an ancient overhead paddle fan blowing a cool breeze to dissipate the sultry Southern evening warmth. Lingering there, they talked of Tildy's memories of Derrik, of Seri's memories of growing up, and the two women even got Carch to tell story after story of his travels through the universe on countless scientific expeditions—something he never did.

He didn't think he'd ever felt as comfortable in his life. No agenda, no expectations. Just relaxing and being himself in the company of two interesting, charming ladies. It was a rare thing in his personal world. He'd spent far too much time in the company of noblemen, space jockeys and grizzled explorers, he decided. Perhaps it was time to hang up his adventurer hat and think about settling down with a good woman. A proper, biddable beauty who would cook him delicious food, bear him a couple of well-mannered children and look after his every need. She'd talk to him of her day and listen to him as he told her about his.

He blinked.

Damn. That sounded boring.

He roused himself and stood. Never mind. He was more of an action man, anyway. "We'd better get going," he said to Seri. "If we're to run down those leads tonight."

The two women looked up in surprise, as though he'd caught them in mid-sentence. Hell, he probably had. Oops.

"But it's the middle of the night," Tildy protested. "What could you possibly do now?"

It wasn't the middle of the night. It was just past eleven. He'd been watching. But no doubt late enough that both the Thin Man and the Palmistry Shoppe would be dark and closed up, their owners gone home. His own establishment, the Old

World Rare and Antique Bookstore, was always the first to close up, promptly at six. Tildy was the only one in the courtyard who lived over her place of business. The other second-floor apartments were let out to various professionals as offices. A lawyer, a tax accountant, an architect. Two interior designers were in the space above the Old World. All of them would have gone home hours ago, as well.

"Trust me," Seri told her aunt, reluctantly rising, "you don't want to know. Go on to bed. We'll be over first thing in the morning." She gave her a hug goodnight and followed him down the stairs.

He made sure the front door was securely locked after them before he turned to her and whispered, "We should start with the—"

A sudden trill of laughter sounded through the courtyard and they both looked over at the Thin Man gallery. Through the mullioned picture windows he saw that lights were blazing and several people stood in a circle among the paintings and statues with martini glasses in their hands.

"They're having a party!" he said with annoyance.

"It's an opening," Seri said, pointing to a poster by the door.

Sure enough, it advertised the opening of a new showing of art deco jewelry. He swore softly.

"We could go in and pretend to be interested in the show. One of us could sneak into the back room while no one is looking."

He wondered briefly if the Imperial Star could pass for Art Deco, then dismissed the thought. That would be too audacious even for the boldest thief. He shook his head. "Too risky. Let's save the gallery for tomorrow. We can do Madam Clarissa's tonight."

Seri frowned when he moved silently along the cobblestone path to the front door of the Palmistry Shoppe. She stayed put so long he didn't think she would come with him.

He'd already pulled latex gloves and his tool kit from his pocket, inserted a pick into the lock and had concentrated on the lock's aura so that the pick rolled the tumblers and had it open before she appeared at his side.

"I can't believe I let you talk me into doing this," she whispered unhappily, donning the gloves he handed her. "If we're caught—"

"We won't be," he assured her, although he really had no control over that part of things. "Not if we're careful." He ushered her inside and closed the door quietly behind them. "And it's not as if we plan to rob the place, or do harm. We only want to reclaim what's ours, if it's here. Nothing more."

She looked unconvinced, but followed his lead as he peered around, adjusting his eyes to the darkness. She banded her arms across her midriff, telegraphing her intent not to touch anything, but nevertheless she edged slowly through the murky shop toward a collection of built-in shelves in the back.

He took out his small flashlight and shone it around. The space was considerably smaller than Tildy's shop, with no clutter of things for sale as in the Second Sun. There was just a round table with two chairs where Clarissa must do her palm reading, an old wooden filing cabinet against one wall and shelves along the back with books and an odd assortment of other items filling them.

"She would hardly leave the necklace lying out for anyone to see—including Aunt Tildy if she happened by," Seri whispered.

"Mmm," he agreed softly, searching through the dark along the black-shadowed walls for an opening. He was rewarded with a door, closed but not locked. "I'll check out the other room," he whispered, and slid through it into a closet-sized space that turned out to be…a storage closet.

He trained his flashlight beam methodically along its

contents—an eclectic mix of junk that must have accumulated across the space of many years. No Imperial Star.

But there was another door. He opened it to find a small, spartan bathroom. A thorough search revealed nothing except a basket with extra tissue and a clean towel.

He was just turning around to return to the main room when he heard a sharp yelp, then a short, piercing scream. As quickly as it started, the scream cut off.

He vaulted through the doors, terrified at what he might find. *"Seri!"*

Chapter 10

Seri slapped both her hands over her mouth to keep herself from screaming again. It was a cat, *only a cat* she assured herself, willing her terror into submission. It was big and black with large amber eyes, and had leapt out of a dark corner of the shop right next to her, running directly to a small cat-sized door tucked next to the entrance of Madam Clarissa's. Already it had melted into the shadows of the courtyard.

"Seri!" Carch dashed into the room and swept her up, crushing her to him as he spun around, searching for danger. "Are you okay?"

"I'm fine. It was just a cat," she said clinging to him, her heart pounding like a bass drum. "But it near scared me to death."

His eyes narrowed for a second sweep around the room. "A cat?"

"It went out the kitty door. There." She pointed down, then shuddered with relief. "Please, can we get out of here now?"

He gave her a squeeze. "The necklace isn't here anyway. Yeah, let's go."

No sooner had they made it back outside and Carch had set the lock than footsteps came running up behind them.

"Did someone scream?" a gruff male voice called. "Hey! What are you doing there?"

Guilt flushed through her.

"Just checking the lock," Carch calmly answered, while she was untangling adrenaline from her chaotic emotions. "Sorry about the scream. My girlfriend thought she saw someone sneaking around this shop. Turned out it was just a cat." He indicated the tiny door next to the big one with a wry smile.

The man frowned and tested the lock himself, grunting when he found it secure. "Cat, eh? Well, you can't be too careful. Had a robbery around here just the other day. The cops have beefed up patrols because of it."

Seri managed to tamp down her jitters and project Carch's same wry tone. "It was my aunt who was robbed. Guess that's why I was so jumpy. Sorry."

The man's eyes lit up. His silver hair reflected the pair of gaslights that illuminated the courtyard. "Your aunt, you say? Well now, I interviewed her earlier for a piece in the *Post and Courier*. John Grodin's the name." He stuck out his hand and she hastened to shake it. "Very nice lady, Miss Tildy."

"Yes, she is," Seri agreed with an uneasy smile, wishing he would just go away. "You're a reporter?"

"A little unusual, isn't it," Carch said conversationally, "doing a whole story about a missing necklace?"

Grodin leaned in. "Took a personal interest in the case," he told Carch meaningfully, as though man-to-man. "On account of Miss Tildy. Seemed mighty upset, bless her. Thought I'd hang around and see if the thieves return to the scene of the crime, as it were."

"You're *watching the courtyard?*" Seri asked, trying her best to mask her dismay. It was a miracle he hadn't caught them breaking into Madam Clarissa's!

"As best I can. Between chasing out a homeless man sleeping in the passageway and the fancy goin's on bringing folks in here at all hours." He jerked a stubbled chin at the Thin Man gallery then shrugged. "What with high society dressing like bums these days, it's getting harder to sort out who belongs and who don't." He turned back to Carch. "So, who did you say you were?"

"I own the Old World Rare and Antique Bookstore," he said, pointing down the path to his place.

She could feel a thrum of tension coming off Carch's body, growing every minute. "We should get home," she said to cut off any more questions from the reporter.

"Yeah. Big day tomorrow." Carch thankfully went along, planting a kiss on her hair as he started to move away.

Before they'd gone two steps, Grodin reached into his rumpled pocket and produced a business card. He handed it to Seri. "Call me if you see anything unusual." He sent Carch a sideways glance. "Anything at all."

"I will," she promised, and they made for the courtyard exit.

She thought about how just this afternoon she would have phoned Grodin in a hot minute, to have him dig up dirt on Carch's background. Now she couldn't wait to escape the reporter, for more reasons than one.

What a difference a few hours made.

Even so, she and Carch argued—okay, discussed in a lively manner—all the way to his place what they should do about Grodin. After getting her adrenaline levels back to normal, Seri had decided they should try to use him. Steer him in whatever direction they thought might be productive. A eporter might get hold of information they had no way of inding out—legally anyway.

Carch didn't want to get within a mile of him.

"I've told you how I feel about the media," he insisted.

"But Grodin is hardly after a story about extraterrestrials," he countered. "He's doing an investigative piece on the obbery. We could help each other."

"Are you sure? Furthermore, how do you know he is who he says he is?" Carch demanded as he parked the Mercedes in his usual spot around the corner from his house. He set the brake and looked at her expectantly.

"What do you mean?"

"Did he show you any identification? If so, I must have missed that part."

"He gave me a business card!"

Carch waved a hand. "Anyone can print those. Doesn't mean it's real. How do you know he was even human?"

"Because—" It suddenly hit her what he was saying. Her jaw dropped. "You can't mean— You think he's an *alien?*"

Carch peered out through the windshield and studied the midnight-quiet street around them. "I honestly don't know. There's at least one Fracian traitor somewhere out there gunning for me. All I'm saying is, we should be careful whom we trust."

"You're telling me you can't recognize someone from your own planet?" she asked incredulously.

"Not if he's shifted to human form. Or to an animal." At her shocked gasp he said, "It's true. That damned cat could have been the assassin for all we know."

"The *cat?*" Now she really was nervous. Anxiously she glanced around the dark neighborhood, searching for movement.

"I'm only half-Galifracian, angel. That's why I had such a hard time shifting. I can do it, but it's a cumbersome process.

Full-blood Fracian nobles can shift far more easily than I, into any kind of humanoid or animal."

"My God," she whispered. "How do you fight something like that?"

"With a great deal of caution," he muttered. "Come on. Let's go."

Reluctant to budge, she slunk lower in her leather seat, feeling goose bumps slide over her flesh. "What if he's out there, waiting for us? What if... Oh, Carch, what if he's inside your house waiting for us? He could have shifted into a housefly, or a spider."

"I guess I should have said *warm-blooded* animal. A mouse is about as small as it gets." He grinned over at her. "And trust me, I've set traps."

"It would serve him right," she said. It was probably hysterics, but she couldn't help the giggle that bubbled up at the image created in her mind of a little green man caught in a mousetrap. But she immediately cringed at her bloodthirsty thought.

"That's my girl." Carch leaned over and gave her a quick kiss.

She straightened like a shot. At his kiss, all at once she remembered...everything. And that they were about to go into his house.

Damn.

They may be in perfect concert about recovering the necklace, but the whole sharing-a-bed thing was not going to work. Not for her, anyway.

"Carch—"

As if sensing where she was headed, he held up a hand. "Stop. Whatever you're about to say, save it until we get in the house." He looked around again. "I'm a sitting duck out here."

It was hard to argue with that. So they piled out and she allowed him to take her hand and scoot down the narrow alley behind his house, slipping through a gate at the rear of his back garden. After pausing a moment to listen intently, they ran to the back door, unlocked it and hurried inside.

She realized they were in the kitchen. Gleaming stainless-steel appliances and glass-fronted cabinets winked in the moonlight that poured in through the window panes. A lingering drift of vanilla scented the night-quiet air.

"All kidding aside, we should be fine in the house," he assured her, locking the door securely behind them. "He knows he still has time. Breaking in would be an act of desperation. If he's been watching us, he also knows we don't have the necklace. He won't risk having you call the police, or being forced to kill you if you got in the way. My death he can get away with if he recovers the Imperial Star. Your death, he'd be severely punished for."

"Because of your rule," she recalled. "The one about no influencing the barbarians."

He kissed her nose. "Natives. We take that particular law very seriously. We should be okay, at least for tonight."

Well, that took care of one worry. She hoped the other would be as easy.

He gazed down at her, then slowly smiled. He tugged her into his arms and the air around them shifted, shimmering with a hum of the delicious electricity she always felt when he touched her.

Oh, lord.

"Why don't we go upstairs and—"

She pulled away and rubbed her hands up and down her arms to rid herself of the tingling feeling. "Carch, we need to talk."

He folded his arms over his broad chest, mirroring her stance. "I've been on Earth long enough to know that means I'm not going to like what you have to say. What is it, angel?"

She paced away from him, attempting to gather her scattered emotions. "I know this might seem a bit like closing the barn door after the horse is gone, but—"

"Huh?"

She gave him a wilted smile and tried a different tack. "Here's the thing. As much as I enjoyed…this afternoon, I just don't think it's a good idea for us to sleep together again."

He tipped his head. "I don't understand. If we both liked having sex, what's wrong with doing it again?" He watched her, waiting.

Flustered that he wouldn't just accept it, she drew herself up. "That's not the point. The point is, I'm *not* going to sleep with you again."

"Why?"

"This afternoon was a mistake. I told you, my curiosity got the better of me. I wanted to know…" She glanced away, embarrassed, then looked back at him. "You're also an incredibly attractive man, Carch. But neither of those things are good enough reasons to…have sex."

"I could make you," he said. The intensity of the statement raised the hairs on her arms.

Inexplicably, her nipples tightened, pulling like strings at her insides. "Yes," she agreed, her voice wobbling. "You could. But you won't."

The corner of his lip curled. "You don't think so? I'm a prince, angel, used to having my slightest whim fulfilled. You really believe I've never done such a thing before, and with relish?"

She swallowed. "No. You're a good man. You wouldn't take anything that wasn't freely given." At least…she didn't think so.

"You gave yourself freely to me this afternoon," he pointed out. He stepped closer. "I claimed you then, Serenity June Woodson. As I took your body, I claimed you as mine."

A rash of goose bumps streaked over her as her doubts blossomed into full panic. She'd convinced herself those words hadn't meant anything. Had she been wrong? Or was he bluffing?

"Maybe on your planet," she brazened. "But on this one it's our own choice to belong to someone or not."

"Oh, you're mine, all right," he said, his lips forming the familiar, all-too-knowing smile. "You proved that to me earlier. Must I prove it to you now?"

"No." He didn't have to. Already her body was betraying her, flushing, tightening, dampening, readying itself for his possession. She might not want to admit it, not to herself, certainly not to him, but she wanted him. Desperately.

And for a blazing moment she couldn't for the life of her remember why she shouldn't just let him have his way. Allow herself to be claimed all over again.

"That's right," he murmured, pulling her stiff body into his embrace. "Let me have my way."

"Don't," she whispered. She could feel his presence in her mind. Not in the usual warm, rolling wave of invasion, but hovering at the fringes of her conscious thought, holding back, listening, biding. Waiting for her to relent. *She was right.* He wouldn't just take her.

"Don't worry about the future, Seri. Allow yourself to enjoy the present."

He pulled her against his broad chest, enveloping her in his strong, corded arms. She could feel his heart beating so close to hers, steady and sure, counting out a rhythm of desire. His hard, thick length pressed into her belly, aroused and insistent.

She bit back a surge of longing. "There should be more involved in having sex than just pleasure," she said, possibly more to convince herself than him.

"Such as?"

She took a deep breath. "Feelings."

There. She'd said it.

And *that* was the biggest reason she couldn't sleep with him again. Not because she didn't have feelings for him. But because she *did.* And they were getting harder and harder to ignore every minute that passed. As crazy as it was, she was falling for Carch. Falling for a man from another planet.

But the idea of a lifetime of lonely solitude and longing for more—like her mother's life, like Aunt Tildy's—was enough to knock Seri back to reality. Carch was *leaving* in less than four days. No way should she allow her heart to become involved. She knew so well what lay down that path. Because men didn't commit. They left.

The object of her dismay studied her for a long moment, the shadows of the night throwing his face into dark relief. Once more, something shifted in the air around them, something deeper, hotter. She shivered, again conscious of the strength and power of his muscular body as he towered over her.

"You believe I have no feelings for you?" He brushed his fingertips lightly over her cheek. A rush of awareness surged through her. "Ah, but I do. A multitude of feelings. Admiration, affection. Faith. I've put my very fate in your hands, by trusting you with the truth about me, by showing you the real me and sharing my most dangerous secrets. I've laid myself at your feet, angel. All I ask in return is that you let me give you pleasure. The greatest pleasure you will ever know."

"But don't you see?" she murmured bleakly, wanting to give in, wanting nothing more than to throw herself into his arms and accept his damned pleasure.

"See what, my sweet?"

"If making love with you is the greatest pleasure I will ever know, then what is to become of me when you leave?"

Chapter 11

Carch's reaction to Seri's plaintively spoken question was so immediate and so visceral that the words tumbled from his mouth before he had a chance to stop them.

"Then come with me."

She blinked up at him in confusion.

"When I leave. Come back with me. To Galifrax."

Her mouth dropped open and she stared at him with the strangest look on her face. For a single, breathless moment he thought she might accept. Then her mouth snapped closed. "Are you insane?"

It was a legitimate question. One he was inclined to answer in the positive, now that he'd had a few seconds to consider his rash offer. What had *possessed* him?

He let out the breath he'd been holding. For surely he *had* been possessed. Possessed by a beautiful, vexatious, independent yet surprisingly vulnerable Earth woman. Just as his father had been, and his grandfather before him. Devils of Taron, it *was* something in his blood. A genetic taint of some sort. It must be. What else could explain this sudden reckless tossing aside of his exciting life of exploration and his more-than-cherished bachelorhood? For an *Earth* woman.

"Possibly," he answered aloud. "But I want you. I don't want to give you up. Come back with me and I'll give you everything your heart desires. Jewels, clothes, a palace of your own. As my mistress, you'll live like a princess. You'll be the envy of all Galifrax. And so will I."

"Your mistress?" she asked, her expression going blank. She took a step backward. "Right. Nice try, spaceman. That might be how things work on your planet, but not here."

Maybe not, but now his offer had been made, the idea took hold of him like a Polerian python that wound itself around his entire body and just wouldn't let go.

He grasped her arm, pulling her back to him. "You don't think I meant it?" he growled, suddenly certain he did.

"Don't be ridiculous," she said, avoiding his gaze. "We've known each other less than twenty-four hours!"

"It took my mother less than twelve to run away with my father."

"They must have gotten along a lot better than we do."

"We get along fine, angel." To show her just how well they got along, he lowered his mouth to hers and kissed her. Long and hard. How much better did she need?

Her initial, rigid resistance melted after a few long seconds. She wanted him. He felt no small amount of satisfaction at that. Because he wanted her, too. Like crazy. More than he'd ever wanted another woman. He couldn't explain it; it annoyed the hell out of him; but there it was. She was a hunger that threatened to overwhelm him. He had to have her. Permanently. But for now, temporarily would do.

He lifted her into his arms and strode through the cave-dark hallway toward the stairs, kissing her the whole way. A matching hunger simmered through her, yet he could also feel her reluctance.

"I told you, you're mine," he whispered in her mouth. "Don't fight it, angel. Don't fight me."

She moaned and clutched his shoulders. "I have to try," she said almost desperately. "You have some kind of terrible, wonderful power over me."

Determination swept through him as he covered her mouth and tasted the sweet nectar of her lips. And he was suddenly terrified that everything he'd done, everything he'd been, hell, his whole life, had been leading him to this one woman.

"We belong together. Be with me now, for my last days on Earth. Let me convince you to come back with me." He paused at the foot of the stairs. Because she was right. He would never take her by force. He would have her consent to enter her body or to take her from her home. Prince or no, there were lines he would not cross, and that was one of them.

"All right," she whispered. "Convince me."

Triumph surged through him, the rush of exhilaration rolling over the shadowy doubts and uncertainties that crowded the edges of his mind. He would have her! He would sink into her heated flesh, revel in her touch and drown in her soft moans.

And as they came together as one, he would show her what it was to belong to him.

He carried her into his room and by the time they reached his bed he had her clothes off. He could see the fine trembling of her body as she lay waiting for him, watching him rid himself of his own.

When he lowered himself between her thighs and onto her welcoming flesh, she whispered, "Let loose your glamour, Carch. I love how it feels against me."

He smiled down at her, pleased. He'd enjoyed it, too—last time's exploration of its subtle pleasures. He closed his eyes and with a shudder willed the tingling glow to radiate from under his skin. Both of their bodies shivered with delight.

Then in a motion, he plunged his full, thick length into her and pulled out again. She let out a high gasp and wrapped her legs around his waist, urging him to thrust back into her. So he did. Over and over and over again, until she dissolved, quivering beneath him.

His glamour still glowed bright, illuminating them and the bed in a wash of sparkling gold. Her eyes fluttered open and she gazed up at him with a languid, half-lidded passion that nearly undid him. His still-hard arousal flexed inside her.

"I won't give you up," he said again, his voice vibrating with a rough urgency even he didn't understand. "I won't."

A great tangle of her emotions rolled through him as her mind fell open to his sensing. But two feelings stood out above all the others.

Her desperate desire for love…and her terror of succumbing to it.

She lifted her hands and gently held his face between them, pulling him down for a kiss. "Love me," she whispered. "Please love me."

His heart filled with an ache he'd never felt before. Other women had pleaded as much, and he'd been unaffected. But this one…

The doubts and uncertainties crowded closer, circling his mind like vultures. Could he love her? Did he even know what love was? Had all those years gallivanting around the universe, all the women, had they dulled his ability to be with just one? To know which one was the right one?

On Galifrax it didn't matter so much. Most people never married, they contented themselves with a series of lovers. If one mistress wasn't right, you moved on to the next. No blame was laid. No stigma attached. Children were loved by all. Everyone did it that way. Except, of course, his parents. They had remained true to each other since the day they'd met forty years ago. Carch had always thought it quaint and archaic, but they loved each other so much it seemed natural, if odd. He had never seen himself in the same role.

Now he wasn't so sure.

But could he do it? Did he know how, even with his parents' example?

Taron, what had he done?

But looking down into Seri's meltingly hopeful face, he knew he would hate himself if he disappointed her.

"I'll try," he whispered back. "I'll try."

Even as Carch gathered her in his arms and started to move over her, filling her anew with his body, giving her exquisite pleasure, Seri knew she had made a mistake.

She should never have used that word.

Love.

Love wasn't something to be trusted.

Oh, she'd always been sure of Aunt Tildy's love. But it was different with men. They were capricious and fickle. Once a man got what he wanted, he'd be gone. The only control a woman had over their feelings was her choice not to let them close enough to *have* any feelings for her. Or her for them.

And this was why. Not fifteen minutes ago he'd asked her to be his mistress, a temporary position in his life—but already he was regretting even that rash offer. She could feel it.

He was making love to her as no one else had, and yet he had withdrawn. Just a little, hardly perceptible. But she was too well-trained as an observer to miss the signs of male discomfort, however small. After all, hadn't she had the textbook example of her father, the man who had said all the right things when he was there, but had nonetheless left her and her mother in a cloud of dust precisely when they needed him most?

"Seri?" Carch murmured, bringing her back to his arms. "Are you still with me?"

Even knowing all that, she sent him up a smile she prayed wasn't wistful, and wrapped her arms tighter around his neck. "I'm with you," she whispered. *For now.* "Please don't stop."

No, Serenity June Woodson was many things, but a coward wasn't one of them. She'd started this affair. And she was determined to experience everything Carch had to offer, as long as he was with her. She knew how it would end, the hurt it would bring when he was gone. But that was days away yet.

So she gave herself up to him, to being Carch Sunstryker's woman, if only for a little while.

Later, when his spacecraft came to carry him away, far, far across the universe, she would face the heartbreak of his loss.

And just pray she survived the pain.

Chapter 12

Carch's internal clock woke him an hour later. It was still dark outside. Time to get up and finish the night's work. He was more determined than ever to find the Imperial Star and fulfill his mission. So he could concentrate on other, more pressing things. Like Seri.

Right or wrong, godsend or disaster, he had asked Serenity June Woodson to come with him back to Galifrax. An honorable man, especially a prince, did not renege on his promises, nor go back on his commitments.

Even though the whole prospect scared him to death.

Without opening his eyes, he reached over to pull her close. After making love, they'd fallen asleep spooned together, and now he was missing her warm body against his.

He felt around, but didn't find her.

Cracking his eyelids open, he glanced over at her side.

No Seri.

Alarm sang through him. He bounded out of bed.

"Seri?" he called. "Angel?"

"I'm in here," she answered from the bathroom. She popped her head out. "Something wrong?" She had put on a pair of jeans and a black T-shirt. Was it his imagination, or did she look nervous?

Confusion swirled through him. "What are you doing?"

"Couldn't sleep. I, uh, thought I'd run over and do a quick reconnaissance of the courtyard."

He frowned. That she couldn't sleep was not a good sign. But the other was of more immediate concern. "You were going without me?"

She had the grace to look guilty. "You were sleeping so peacefully, and… Carch, the bad guy isn't after me. I'll be fine."

"The hell you will," he growled, stalking over to scowl down at her, hands on hips. Unfortunately, she didn't look the least bit intimidated. *Infuriating woman.* "You go *nowhere* without me. Understand?"

Her brows shot up, as did her chin. "I'm a grown woman, Carch. I'll go where I wish and with—or without—whom I please."

He didn't miss the subtext. Or was he imagining that? No, probably no more than he'd imagined her unease. They'd had a very emotional night on a lot of levels. Was she running as scared as he?

Blowing out a breath, he did a mental backpedal. He spread his arms, inviting her in. "Come here," he said.

After a heartbeat's hesitation, she came to him. He folded her into his embrace, laid his cheek against the top of her hair and drew in the sweet spice of her womanly scent and the lingering musk of his lovemaking. It was a powerful combination. One that marked her as his woman. He liked the sensation of protectiveness it had begun evoking within him.

"Angel, I don't want you to get hurt. Would you begrudge me whatever protection I can give you?"

"No. Of course not. I'm just…"

"Just what?" He lifted her face and looked into her eyes. "Terrified and running away from me?"

Her shoulders notched down. "Yeah. I guess I am."

"Well, don't. Aside from not being safe, running away is not necessary. I'm not going to kidnap you and spirit you off to another planet against your will. I promise."

That earned a faint smile. "Too bad. At least that way I wouldn't have to choose."

He smiled back. "Sorry. I can't. Another one of—"

"Your stupid Galifracian rules," she completed with a wry nod. "Should have known."

"Not so stupid," he said somberly.

"No, I know. Sorry. A moment of weakness." She sighed. "This isn't easy for me, you know. Not any of it."

"You're an incredibly brave woman. Don't let anyone tell you different. Yourself included."

She smiled wonderingly up at him and murmured, "How is it you make me feel so out of control, yet so safe and secure, all at the same time?"

He gave her a tender look. "At least it's not all bad, then, things between us," he said, and kissed her.

"No," she said so quietly he had to strain to hear. "If it weren't so good it wouldn't be nearly this scary."

And that, he thought with a sigh, summed things up in a nutshell.

For a moment they stood in each other's arms, listening to their hearts beating in alternate rhythms. He deliberately stayed out of her mind, not really wanting to know what was going on in there.

"So," he said, thinking he'd better change the subject

before he did something else he'd regret—not that he exactly regretted anything he'd done…yet. "You were leaving to check out the Second Sun courtyard?"

She pulled away and nibbled on her lower lip. "Yeah."

"Good idea," he said, surprising her. He headed for the bathroom to splash his face and get dressed. "If the coast is clear, we'll search the Thin Man, okay?" he called out.

"Okay." She didn't sound happy about it.

"Maybe you should stay here. I can go alone," he suggested when he emerged, hoping against hope she'd agree. He didn't believe his grandfather's enemies would dare kill her outright, but any number of other things could go wrong. Not the least of which was getting arrested.

Her mouth took on a mulish slant. "No way. If you go, I go."

He didn't bother arguing. He knew he'd lose.

"All right," he said, grabbing his tools from the dresser. "Then let's roll."

All was quiet when Carch and Seri reached their first stop, the Old World Bookstore. Quiet and dark.

He quickly unlocked the front door and they went in. After flipping on a single light over his desk in back, they made their way to the rear door that led into the courtyard. That way, if they ran into anyone, their cover would be that they had returned for something Carch had forgotten at the bookstore and had heard strange noises coming from the Thin Man.

For several minutes they watched the deserted courtyard. The weather played accomplice, having deposited a thick, low-lying fog over the rooftops. The only movement in the sultry mist was the occasional fluttering of leaves from the lush foliage crowding the small garden. Nothing else stirred. Even the birds were silent.

"Grodin?" Carch ventured to call out softly into the stillness in case the reporter was hidden in the shadows. "You around?"

No answer. He must have given up and gone home. Small blessings.

Satisfied they were alone, Carch silently signaled Seri to follow him outside and down the cobblestone path to the Thin Man, which was next door.

Unlike Madam Clarissa's, the Thin Man had an alarm system. Not terribly sophisticated, luckily. Once he had defeated the lock and they'd slipped inside, it took only a moment for him to feel his way to the correct combination on the keypad using the wear pattern on the buttons and the residual energy that hovered above them, resetting the alarm.

That seemed to impress Seri—in a sardonic kind of way. Pulling her latex gloves from her pocket, she shook her head and muttered something about aliens and nothing being safe.

Oh, well. At least they were in.

He had a feeling about these suspects. David and Alan, the owners of the gallery, had motive to steal the necklace, and from everything Tildy said, the means and opportunity as well. With any luck, anyone who was idiot enough to rob their next-door neighbor would be idiot enough to keep their ill-gotten gains right in their own place of business.

Keeping to the walls of the large, open space that comprised the main gallery, they sneaked around to the side with a locked door to the back business area. Once through the door, they pulled out their flashlights and swept them over the first room. They were in a small sitting area with sleek art-deco furnishings. A simple wave-shaped desk—no drawers—sat in one corner, and a sofa grouping and a low, polished coffee table took up most of the other space. Nowhere obvious to hide anything. Wordlessly they split up and worked their way around the room, peeking under the many paintings on the wall, looking for a safe.

Nothing.

Carch indicated to Seri that she should take the powder room, then carefully opened a second door, which led to the office. By the time he'd thoroughly gone through the many drawers in a spectacular burled walnut desk that took up most of the space, Seri joined him.

He looked up. "Anything?"

She shook her head. "Just an incredibly gorgeous inlaid marble vanity I'd kill for."

He smiled. When they got back to Galifrax he'd have one made for her. The artisans on his planet were unmatched, and he could afford to indulge his woman.

With a start he realized what he was thinking about. *Setting up housekeeping with her.* He should have been disconcerted, but instead he felt an almost disquieting sense of anticipation.

Damned if he didn't *want* to set up housekeeping with her.

When had that happened?

"Want to start on the file cabinet?" he asked in a whisper, to distract himself from his unexpected thoughts. He could think about the implications of his little revelation later.

Together they searched the rest of the office and again turned up nothing. The only thing left was the safe that must surely be under one of the stylized paintings of long, elegantly posed ladies. They found it behind the fourth one, and after a few passes Carch swung the safe's door open.

When he trained his flashlight inside, they hit pay dirt. Right on top of a pile of bundled money and a business checkbook lay a stunning color photograph of the Imperial Star of Galifrax.

Seri gasped, and grabbed his arm. "That's it! My God, you were right!"

The gold and gemstone necklace was brilliantly lit in the photo, posed against a backdrop of luxuriant black velvet. Even on paper it sparkled like a galaxy on fire.

She looked up at him. "It *was* them. David and Alan. They must have it here somewhere!"

Swiftly they examined the contents of the safe. No necklace.

Carch swore harshly under his breath. "Could we have missed another hiding place?" He glanced around the office. "Let's go through everything again. This time keep your eyes open for any papers that might tell us what else they could have done with it, in case it really isn't here."

It wasn't. They spent the better part of an hour meticulously searching every nook and cranny for a possible hidey hole. All in vain. The last thing Carch did was retrieve the photo and flip it over, hoping they'd written some clue to its whereabouts on the back. The number *473* was scrawled in blue ink. Nothing more.

"What the hell does that mean?" he ground out.

Frustration pulled at every nerve in his body. So damn close! To find concrete evidence but not the actual necklace had not been in the plan.

"What could they have done with the thing?" he growled, quietly closing the last desk drawer but wanting nothing more than to slam the hell out of it.

Seri was still looking at the photo. She shook her head and carefully replaced it on the pile of money in the safe. "Maybe they already sold it." She took out the checkbook that had sat under the photo and ran her flashlight beam down the check register inside. "Hmm. Maybe not. No large deposit has been recorded since the robbery. Nothing paid to a courier or delivery company, either."

"Maybe they're not as amateur as they appeared at first glance," he conceded. "Okay, if you had a valuable piece of jewelry, where would you hide it?"

"I'd keep it in a safety deposit box at the bank," she said without hesitation, then blinked and looked down at the checkbook in her hand. "Like maybe this bank. City Bank of Charleston."

He met her eyes with a sinking feeling in the pit of his stomach. "Damn."

"The number on back of the photo—473. I'll bet it's the box number," she said.

"I'll bet you're right." Which didn't make him feel one bit better.

Breaking into an art gallery was one thing. Breaking into a bank was quite another.

Gods of Moradth! Now what?

Seri looked at her watch. "We better get out of here. It'll start getting light out soon."

"Yeah," he agreed, and led the way back out into the main gallery and then to the door they'd entered from the courtyard. He made short work of locking up, and they hurried the few yards down the cobblestone path toward the Old World Bookstore.

Suddenly Seri stopped dead in her tracks. He halted and followed the direction of her horrified gaze to the center of the courtyard. Two large, luminescent green eyes stared out at them from the darkness.

It was the black cat.

Chapter 13

"Is that the same cat?" Carch asked Seri with a frown.

"Would it matter?"

She sidled behind him and pressed her body close to his back. Not that she was afraid of cats. Okay, maybe this one. But only because it could be an alien assassin in disguise.

She choked back a desperate laugh. Listen to her! This time she'd gone completely mad.

"No, I suppose it wouldn't," Carch murmured. "A shapeshifter can easily change his spots."

"Talk to it," she whispered. When he just gave her an incredulous look over his shoulder, she stuck her head out from behind him and yelled at the cat, "Go away. Leave us alone! We didn't find the damn necklace, okay?"

The cat just sat and stared at her with its slanted blue eyes. Eyes that looked eerily like Carch's, the one time she'd seen them in their true form. She swallowed that thought.

"Scat!" she hissed. "Before I call animal control and have your furry butt locked up at the pound."

A hollow threat. Animal control didn't open until at least eight o'clock, and even if she had the beast scooped up, if he was a shapeshifter, getting away would be a minor inconvenience. And if he was a real cat, Seri would feel guilty for the rest of her life about having an innocent kitty tossed in animal jail.

The cat's only reaction was to stretch leisurely, turn and slowly saunter away, ducking under Aunt Tildy's fragrant flowering gardenia to disappear.

"An interesting strategy, telling him we didn't find the necklace," Carch said dryly. But he was grinning. "Think he believed you?"

She bristled, feeling more than a little foolish. "Hey, he left, didn't he?"

A voice came from behind them. "There was another one?" They spun around to see the reporter John Grodin standing in the mouth of the arched passageway.

"Another cat?" Carch asked, brow raised.

"That's who you were talking to?" Grodin looked surprised. "A cat? Thought it was another bum. Chased one out of the passage just now. Damned homeless people," he grumbled. "Should get a job like everyone else."

Charleston didn't have a big homeless problem downtown. Seri certainly didn't recall ever seeing a homeless person in the courtyard or the passageway before yesterday. And this was the second occasion Grodin had mentioned one hanging around.

A chill went down her spine. Maybe she was concerned about a four-legged assassin when she should be more worried about a two-legged one.

Or…maybe there were *two* traitors.

"So, y'all been out dancing till dawn?" Grodin asked.

"What? Oh. Yeah, something like that," she answered him distractedly.

"Kind of early for you, too," Carch remarked.

"Nah. Statistically, most crimes are committed between six and eight in the morning."

"Really?"

The idea of *two* assassins being after them had caused a thread of panic to wind through her. She yanked it back long enough to grab Carch's hand and tug him toward the bookstore just as Grodin answered.

"They've done studies. I'm just getting the jump on him."

"Well, nice seeing you again," she told him, sidling off. "And good luck."

They'd just made it to the bookshop door and Carch had opened it for her when Grodin called after them in one of those fake Colombo afterthoughts, "Oh…meant to tell you folks, I heard from my contact at the Charleston PD that they've ordered a background check on everyone doing business in the courtyard. In connection with the investigation of your aunt's robbery. Just wanted to let you know." He smiled cordially and waved.

She felt a ripple of irritation radiate from Carch's body. She had to practically drag him into the Old World.

"Great," he ground out. "Just freaking great. One more thing to worry about."

She pushed him with both hands toward the middle of the maze of floor-to-ceiling bookshelves that filled the bookshop. "I'd say it makes two more things," she corrected, barely keeping the panic at bay now. "Three, if you count the damn cat."

She stopped when they reached a spot deep in the stacks of books that wasn't visible through the windows from any direction. He turned to her. "That's not making me feel better," he muttered.

She crossed her arms over her abdomen to keep them from shaking. "It wasn't meant to."

Things were spinning out of control fast. Not that she'd ever had any real control over this unbelievable situation. Up until now she'd had such a feeling of unreality, the horrifying danger of it all hadn't really sunk in. But that had all changed.

"What are we going to do? If the police find out you don't even *have* a background—"

Carch slashed his fingers through his hair. "They won't. They're going to think I'm lying."

That got her attention. Though she had a feeling the answer would undoubtedly only make things worse, she asked, "Why?"

"I bought the bookstore shortly after I first arrived on Earth, as a cover. Cash, no questions asked. I probably shouldn't have, but it was for sale and the situation—being here on the courtyard so close to Tildy—was too perfect to pass up. Gave me a reason to hang around."

She had wondered why he'd bought the store—and how. "Okay. But that's a good thing. He'll know you're legit."

"Except, a few days later I signed over ownership to the long-time manager."

For a second, surprise pushed aside her humming nerves. "You mean Mr. Smalls?"

Abel Smalls had already been working a long time at the Old World Rare and Antique Bookstore when she'd come to live with Aunt Tildy as a teenager. He wasn't quite as ancient as the books he loved so much, but nearly.

Carch spread his hands. "The man's been earning minimum wage his whole life just because he wants to do something he loves. He's got no pension, no savings to speak of. He deserves a break. He doesn't know it yet but after I leave, documents will be delivered to him giving him legal ownership of the shop free and clear."

Seri gazed at Carch, her fear temporarily forgotten as her heart swelled with pride and warmth over this wonderful, generous man. "You really are something, spaceman," she whispered, and stretched up on her toes to give him a kiss.

His arms went around her and he returned the kiss with exquisite gentleness. "So are you, Earth girl." He sighed. "So, you going to bail me out when the cops throw me in jail?"

"Don't worry. There'll be a paper trail showing you bought it. Besides, I thought you said Grodin might not be human? If he's the traitor, the cops are the least of your worries."

He let out an exasperated breath. "Taron, woman. Are you deliberately trying to make me more paranoid?"

Which gave them *another* suspect to count. And just like that, the fear was back. "What are we going to do, Carch? My God, the traitor could be anyone. How will we—"

"Shhh," he soothed with a squeeze. "Let me worry about the traitor. Right now, let's just concentrate on getting the necklace back. At least we have an idea where to look for it. I call that progress."

She forced herself to let him go, then took a deep cleansing breath and let it out. "You're right. It is."

"There isn't anything else we can do tonight. Let's go home."

At his last words, a funny feeling spun through her heart. *Home.* Strange how she'd lived for almost five years in Phoenix and it still didn't feel like home, but a few hours at Carch's place and it felt as though she belonged there.

Or, rather, with him.

It was a frightening thought. Almost more frightening than being chased by a deadly assassin. Because if you survived the assassin's bullet you would still be you, the same person as before. But regardless of what happened with Carch…after being with him, she would never be the same again. Nor would her heart.

In two short days, Carch Sunstryker had changed her, and her poor heart, forever.

And that was the scariest thought of all.

Seri walked with Carch up the grand staircase to his bedroom. When he took her hand firmly in his and led her inside, she offered no coy pretense of resistance. She wanted to be with him and there was no use denying it.

She'd made up her mind. She could not go to Galifrax as his mistress. The Fracian custom of moving easily from one partner to the next over a lifetime was exactly why she'd avoided relationships with men. She couldn't accept that idea.

But as long as Carch was here on Earth, she would be at his side, for good and bad.

And this part was definitely good.

Very good.

It had been a long, eventful day and they were both exhausted. But that didn't stop them from making love again. And this time Seri truly felt they were making love.

The air still crackled with their attraction and shimmered with desire whenever they touched. Their kisses were still as deep and drugging, their joining as intensely pleasurable.

But something had changed profoundly between them.

A feeling inside. At least, inside her.

And it wasn't Carch's presence in her mind. Well, it partly was. But tonight he brought a different presence than before, with a purely emotional quality that filled her with equal measures of heat and yearning. Yearning to belong. To him.

Only to him.

Unfortunately, that was not possible. He didn't want her forever. He only wanted her as his mistress, not his wife.

Something she could not accept. Not if he expected her to go to another planet with him.

But she didn't allow herself to ask about the future, or even to think about it; she only wanted to revel in the here and now. Who knew what tomorrow would bring? But tonight was real.

Tonight she was his.

And if that was all she got, she didn't want to waste a single minute of their time worrying about the future.

A future they could not share.

The delicious smell of coffee and something sweet and baked finally drove Seri from an all-too-short sleep.

"Morning, sleepyhead."

"Mnnnmmmph," she protested as she forced her leaden eyelids up. She glanced at the clock. Nine-forty-five.

Carch set a loaded tray down on the foot of his king-sized bed. Suddenly, she was wide awake. He was still naked. Gloriously naked. Wonderfully, sinfully naked. But the fragrance from the tray was glorious, wonderful and sinful, too. Her eyes strayed from his tempting body to the tempting tray.

Decisions, decisions.

She looked back at him consideringly.

"Don't even think about it," he said with a curve to his perfect lips. "We have things to do this morning."

She smiled innocently. "Think about what?" She batted her eyelashes when it became more than obvious that he was thinking the same thing.

"You," he said, smacking her smartly on the rear, "are a very bad influence."

"Ouch!" She pouted. "Who says I wasn't thinking about the coffee and—" She peered at the delectable pastrylike confections on the tray. "What are those anyway?"

"Beignets," he said. "My grandfather took Tildy for a weekend in New Orleans while he was here. He still raves about them. When I got here I talked the bakery down the street into making some and they were so popular they added them to their inventory."

She picked one up and bit into it. "Omigod," she said around the generous layer of powdered sugar. *Talk about sinful.* "These are great."

He slid onto the bed next to her with a grin and helped himself to a big one. "They are kind of tasty."

Suddenly she scowled over at him. "Oh! That is so not fair!"

He paused in mid bite. "What?"

"You never get fat, do you? You can just shapeshift away the extra pounds!"

He was smart enough to stop grinning. "Um. I guess so. Never been a problem before. So," he quickly said, "what's our strategy for the bank this morning?"

She knew exactly what he was doing, but figured this was more important than giving him a hard time, as amusing as that was, so she turned her thoughts to business.

"The safety deposit boxes are usually locked up in a special vault," she said. "And even if it's possible to access them, we'll still somehow have to arrange to be in the vault alone."

"What if we ordered our own safety deposit box? They'd have to let us inside the vault then, right?"

She licked sugar off her fingers and nodded thoughtfully. "Yeah. That could work." She looked up. "Then what?"

"Then I open box 473 and pray the necklace is there."

"And you'll take it?"

"No, I'll wait and exchange it for the substitute I'm having made. Remember? It should be ready any day now."

She smiled. "So if we're lucky they'll never even know."

"Brilliant, eh?"

Her smile dimmed a little. "If it works. Do you really think you'll be able to open the box without a key?"

"Unless it's a very complicated mechanism, cracking it shouldn't be too hard. The bigger problem will be the security camera. I assume they'll have one watching us."

Damn. She hadn't thought of that. "No doubt."

"Well, let's get dressed and give it a try. Hell, what's the worst that can happen?"

She gazed over at him and her heart gave a painful squeeze. The worst?

Unfortunately, she could think of any number of unpleasant scenarios.

But the one that suddenly frightened her the most was that once they recovered the necklace, Carch Sunstryker would take off for home. He'd have to go, with or without her. To save his family.

Would he repeat his offer to her to come with him? Or had that just been an empty invitation that he'd later regretted?

If he did ask her again, would she have the courage to give up everything to go with him? Her home, her job, her friends, her aunt? Even the birds and trees and the familiar oceans and continents of her own planet? Everything? For a man she barely knew?

My God, if she went with him, she would lose control over every single aspect of her life! Could she do it?

She didn't think so. The whole notion was crazy insane. Illogical. Unreasonable and impetuous. Everything she'd worked so hard to avoid her whole life. Everything she was not. Not to mention scary as hell.

But if he asked her and she told him no…would she find herself living a life of solitude and regret, like Aunt Tildy, without Tildy's good reason for staying…wishing she'd been brave enough to follow her heart and accept?

Who knew the right answer?

Good thing he hadn't asked.

"Yeah," she said with a sigh, and looked up into his expectant blue eyes. "What's the worst that could happen?"

Chapter 14

The plan worked.

As far as it went.

Carch and Seri got to the City Bank of Charleston and arranged to rent a safety deposit box. A clerk signed them up with a flurry of paperwork, then accompanied them into the vault which contained a sturdy table and two chairs—and a security guard posted outside the thick bars of the entrance gate. Using the keys, they pulled out their new box—number 289—and the guard turned his back discreetly as the clerk left them alone with the box on the table.

They had agreed earlier not to say anything aloud that might raise suspicion from whomever might be listening, either electronically or in person. So Carch engaged in meaningless chitchat with Seri as he made a careful survey of the inside of the vault.

Just as he'd feared, there was a security camera lurking in

the corner just under the ceiling and it was aimed right at the wall of numbered boxes.

The bank was a small branch, so the box numbers only went up to 500. He wandered around the room for a few minutes while Seri fussed with the decoy documents they'd brought to put into their own box. Casually, he placed his hand against box 473, trying to appear as though he was just leaning against the wall as he waited for her. Keeping perfectly still, he closed his eyes and concentrated on the lock beneath his palm. He could feel the outline of the mechanism's energy. Opening it would be tricky, but not impossible. It took two keys, with the interaction of the two sets of gears springing the lock and opening the box. Given enough time, he could do it.

After deciding the types of picks best suited to the task, he removed his hand. "Almost finished?" he asked pleasantly.

She glanced up and he gave an almost imperceptible nod. "Yep," she said. "All done."

They called the guard to lock up their box, and left the bank. The branch was only a few blocks away from Queen Street, so they headed on foot to the Second Sun where Tildy was expecting them for lunch.

"What do you think?" Seri asked him when they'd walked a block or so. "Is it possible?"

He jetted out a breath. "On my part, yes. But it'll take time, and that camera will be a problem. We'll need a diversion."

"A diversion?"

"To distract whoever is watching the security monitors."

"Ah. So they'll be watching whatever's going on and won't see you break into the box," she mused. "Think it'll work?"

"You have a better idea?"

Unfortunately she didn't.

He thought about what kind of a diversion they could create as they walked down King Street, weaving through the throngs of shorts-clad tourists and fashionable Charlestonians heading out for a leisurely lunch or an afternoon of shopping. The sun was directly overhead and the temperature the typical high of early summer in the Lowcountry, but a nice breeze was blowing in from the Battery so it wasn't uncomfortably humid.

Seri was looking even more beautiful than usual in a sleeveless summer dress in the exact cool, greenish-blue color of the Eldor Sea back home. The city of Eldor, where he lived, was perched on an expanse of tall, white cliffs rimming the sea, and the royal castle where his family resided was built on a precipice overlooking the crashing green-blue waves.

Thinking of home and family made his heart ache.

What if he failed in his mission? What if something awful happened to them because of his failure? In that case, he hoped the traitor killed him first. He wouldn't want to go on living if his family suffered because of him.

He glanced over at the woman by his side—the lovely woman he wanted more than anything to take home with him. But that wouldn't be possible if he didn't recover the Imperial Star of Galifrax first.

He squared his shoulders and clamped his jaw determinedly. Failure was not an option. He *would* succeed in opening the safety deposit box, and the necklace *would* be inside.

But to accomplish that, they needed a diversion.

A good one.

Apparently he and Seri both came to the same conclusion at the same time.

"It'll have to be Tildy," they said in unison, then glanced at each other somberly.

"I don't like involving her," Seri said.

"Neither do I, but I don't think we have a choice."

They stopped along with a small crowd of tourists for a

red light. Two white-helmeted policemen rode by on tall, brown horses.

Seri watched them clip-clop past. "Could we tell the police what we found?" she asked. "So they'd get a warrant to have the box opened legally?"

Carch had already considered that idea and dismissed it. Aside from not wanting to get within a mile of a law-enforcement officer if he didn't have to, there was the whole logistics of the conversation.

"By telling them what?" he asked mildly as they crossed the street. "That we just happened to break into the Thin Man gallery, and we found a picture of the necklace in the safe we accidentally cracked?"

She grimaced. "I see your point. But I still don't like involving anyone else. Especially Aunt Tildy."

"Me neither." They entered the courtyard passageway and walked along the cobblestone path leading to the Second Sun. "Well, let's just hope she—"

"Hey!" a gruff voice suddenly called out. Or rather, *up.* "Watch where you're goin', will ya!"

Carch halted just before stumbling over a grubby man who was lying propped up against the brick wall of the building between Madam Clarissa's and the Second Sun. She recognized him from when she'd first arrived yesterday. His hair was over his collar and his face was unshaven. He wore dirty camo pants and a wrinkled linen duster over his torn T-shirt despite the heat, and he had an open bottle in a paper sack in one hand. He must also be the homeless "bum" Grodin had talked about last night.

"Sorry," Carch said, looking the man over with more distaste than alarm. He didn't appear to be an assassin. But you never knew. "Why don't you try the bench over there?" Carch pointed to the beautiful wooden garden bench in the center of the courtyard, then extended his hand down to the man to help him up—and at the same time do a quick mind-probe. "The ground can't be all that comfortable."

The man stared at his proffered hand. Seri was in turn staring at the man, her eyes narrowed.

"Don't mind if I do," the man said with the feigned dignity of a drunk, waving his paper-bag-clad bottle to keep his balance as he clumsily grabbed Carch's hand.

As soon as their hands touched, Carch subtly rolled mental feelers into the man's mind. To his shock he slammed up against a fortresslike strength and single-minded purpose. But what it was he didn't get the chance to find out. The man stumbled—or pretended to—and the contact was broken.

"You're a cop!" Seri blurted out, jolting both Carch and the other man. "Undercover! Aren't you?" she demanded with an undertone of outrage.

Alarm shot through Carch; his whole body went rigid.

The man's face hardened. "Shhh! Lower your voice." He straightened, looking disgusted. And not in the least drunk. "Damn it! How the *hell* did you make me? What gave it away?"

Carch was wondering the same thing. He peered at Seri who stood with her fists parked on her hips.

"Your shoes." They all glanced down at the cop's shoes. "It struck me last time I ran into you. No homeless person wears hundred-and-fifty-dollar Air Jordans." She waved a hand over the front of him. "And the rest of your clothes. You rubbed dirt on them but they're all new and of good quality. Shoot, the little inspection sticker is still on the sleeve of your coat."

The man scowled in irritation and grabbed his sleeve to check. "Damn it," he muttered.

"But the kicker is your smell."

The cop glanced up. "I do not smell," he gritted out indignantly.

Her eyebrows flickered. "That's the problem."

Despite the fact that Carch had noted most of these things himself, he was still pretty impressed with Seri's powers of quick observation. Score another point for the science teacher.

"Who are you?" Carch asked the cop. "What are you doing here?"

After giving a furtive glance around the courtyard, the man reached into his inside pocket for a thin wallet and flipped it open. The name on it was Seton Williams and he was indeed a detective with the Charleston Police Department.

Devils of Taron, had they found out about him? But how?

"I'm doing surveillance on the owners of the Thin Man Art Deco Gallery," Williams said in a low voice. "They're under investigation. Have you seen any unusual activity inside the gallery?"

Carch was too surprised and relieved to react other than letting out an uneven breath.

"Under investigation for what?" Seri asked, all business.

"I'm not at liberty to discuss that."

"They stole my aunt's necklace," she announced. "It's very valuable."

Carch winced at her disclosure as Williams gazed at her with stark interest. "The robbery here reported a couple of days ago?" She nodded. "You have proof of that?" he asked.

"No," Carch said quickly, trying to signal her to keep her mouth shut. "No proof."

She ignored him. "I saw a photograph. Of the necklace. In their studio yesterday. Can you get a warrant?"

"Based on a photograph?" After a slight hesitation, Williams shook his head. "I doubt it's enough. And I'm not going to blow my whole case tipping our hand. This thing is way larger than one necklace, no matter how valuable."

"How large?" Seri asked.

"Please," he said, glancing over at the Thin Man Gallery, "you better leave now, before anyone gets suspicious." He handed her a business card he fished out from his duster pocket. "Call if you get solid proof they stole the necklace. Otherwise, do me a favor and pretend I'm invisible, like everyone else does."

With that he made a rude comment in a loud voice, swung his bottle to his lips and dropped unsteadily back to the ground, sprawling out on the cobblestones.

Just then, Carch spotted Madam Clarissa watching them from behind the curtain of the Palmistry Shoppe.

He grabbed Seri's arm and pulled her inside the Second Sun before the old busybody could come out and waylay them.

"Are you nuts?" he demanded when they were in the shop and well out of range of prying eyes and ears. "Telling that detective about the photo? What if he'd asked for more specifics? Like how we found it?"

"I thought it was worth the risk to see if he could get a warrant for that safety deposit box. I don't like breaking the law."

"I'm not in the habit myself. But in this case—" He cut off with a low curse. "I have no other choice, Seri, but you don't have to go with me. I'll figure out some other way to get to it."

"No." She put her hand on his arm. "I'm committed to helping you, Carch, come what may."

His heart melted and he kissed her. "You can't know how much that means to me, angel."

"Hello, you two!" Aunt Tildy's chipper voice called as she emerged with a jingle from behind the black velvet curtain of the back salon where her tarot table was located. Her gaze landed on their embrace and first surprise, then a bleak expression passed over her face. "Oh, dear. I thought… That is, I never thought—"

"It's okay, Aunt Tildy," Seri said quietly. "You needn't worry about me. At least not where Carch is concerned."

Tildy let out a heartfelt sigh. "I just..." Her misty eyes searched him and Seri, whom he still held in his arms.

"I know," Seri said softly, glancing up at him then back to her aunt. "Believe me, I know."

Carch felt like a class-A jerk. He wanted her to come back with him to Galifrax. But—as what? He wasn't ready to make her any promises. Especially ones he might not be able to keep. He wanted her with him, but he wasn't the settling-down type. What if it didn't work out?

He thought about the envelope addressed to Tildy that he had stashed in a drawer at his house. From King Derrik, with instructions to give it to her the day before Carch left—but only if he got the necklace. What did it say? Was it an invitation for Tildy to join Derrik on Galifrax? If it was, it might make his decision to press Seri that much easier. At least she'd have her aunt with her, if things fell apart.

Soon, he promised himself. Soon he'd have the necklace back in his possession. Then he'd be able to think about what he really wanted. And make a decision one way or another.

Take her or leave her?

Leave her or take her?

It was driving him crazy. But what if he made the wrong choice? And was stuck with it for the rest of his life...

But first he had to get the damned necklace—or there wouldn't be a choice to make.

Chapter 15

All things considered, Aunt Tildy took the revelation of Carch's mission and their request for her help at the bank pretty well. Seri was glad Carch hadn't told her the worst parts of the story—specifically, him being shot, and the extent to which her beloved Derrik would suffer for gifting her with the forbidden necklace if it wasn't recovered. He'd told just enough of the truth to convince her aunt the Imperial Star must be found, and that she must content herself with the replica Carch was having made.

Still, Seri had the distinct, uncomfortable impression that he'd left something out. Something even she didn't know about. But honestly, things were bad enough that if he didn't want to tell her, she really didn't want to know.

Despite taking the news with admirable stoicism, Aunt Tildy chose to retire right after lunch for a nap, visibly shaken.

Seri gave her a long hug before her aunt went to her room. "It'll be all right, Aunt Tildy," she reassured her, hating the tremors she felt in the older woman's body. "I promise."

"I know, dear. I'm happy to help. The important thing is that you find the Imperial Star. That's the only promise I need. I'll be fine."

She wondered how much her aunt guessed of that which remained unsaid. She might be eccentric, but she was definitely not stupid. For her aunt's sake, Seri was determined to do everything in her power to make sure the necklace was returned to King Derrik so nothing terrible befell him or his family.

She and Carch watched her aunt walk slowly out of the living room, then turned to each other.

"I almost wish she'd said she wouldn't help us at the bank," Carch murmured, obviously worried about Tildy.

"She's stronger than she looks," Seri said, even though she agreed with him. "It's a good plan. They can't arrest her for dropping a jar of coins all over the floor and having hysterics."

"I suppose not." Carch's reluctant eyes sought the hallway down which Tildy had disappeared. Warmth and admiration seeped through Seri's insides at his concern. Despite his occasional arrogance, he really was a caring person.

"Why don't you call the jeweler and see if the replacement is ready?" she suggested, anxious to get everything in place so they could do the switch and get this whole thing over with. Once they had the Imperial Star in their possession they could relax a bit. Not completely, of course. But enough to focus on other things for a while.

Like the future. Her future. *Their future.*

But until they got their hands on the necklace, any kind of future was an unknown quantity. Best not to think about it. Not yet, anyway. Not until they'd gotten past the next few hours.

* * *

"My God, it's beautiful."

Seri held the replica necklace up to the sunlight streaming through the jeweler's window. It was identical to the original in every way that she could see. Gemstones glittered and winked as hundreds of polished facets reflected the brilliant light. The gold star setting glowed a lustrous yellow beneath them, looking so much like Carch's golden glamour that she glanced up at him and smiled.

He was watching her with a look that made a thrill run through her whole body. It was the look of a man who wanted to shower her with jewels and gaze at her for hours wearing his gifts and nothing more.

She handed the necklace back to the jeweler. "An amazing piece."

"Thank you," he said. "The design is extraordinary. I've been trying to pry out of Mr. Sunstryker who did the original. I'd love to hire this person."

Carch laughed genially. "Unfortunately, he's long gone. I told you, this is a replica of an ancient piece I found on my travels in the East."

"Not with all those facets, it's not," the man observed with the certainty of an expert. "That takes modern tools to achieve. But I don't blame you for keeping the designer a secret. However, if you ever change your mind…"

After he took care of the transaction, Carch put the necklace around her neck and clasped it. If the traitor was tailing them, they didn't want to be seen carrying anything out of the shop. She adjusted her clothing—after lunch she'd deliberately changed into a skirt and a dark, collared blouse—so the necklace didn't show beneath.

"Good?"

Carch nodded. "Not a hint."

"Shall we go directly to the bank?" she asked as they exited the shop.

He put his arm around her shoulder as they walked down the street. "No, we'll have to coordinate with Tildy first."

She jetted out a breath. "Right. Forgot about that." What was wrong with her? She had never forgotten important details like this. She must be more nervous than she thought.

Sensing her disquiet, Carch pulled her close to his side. "Don't worry. This will work. It has to."

She hoped to heaven he was right. The sleepless night and looking over her shoulder all day was beginning to wear on her. Along with the other stuff…

No. Not thinking about it.

"We should give Aunt Tildy another hour for her nap. What can we do in the meantime?" she asked.

"Same thing?" He gave her a look that said he didn't have sleeping in mind.

She rolled her eyes. "Good grief, Carch. Are all extraterrestrials this obsessed with sex?"

"Not an obsession." He grinned. "Just a healthy appetite. Given the right woman."

He was just teasing, but the words hung in the air, giving her goose bumps. The right woman for sex, sure. But what about more? What about—

No. Not thinking about it.

"Well, I think we should—"

Suddenly, a kid on a skateboard appeared, zooming down the sidewalk straight toward them. They jumped apart to avoid a collision. Then just as suddenly she felt strong hands grab at her and before she realized what was happening, the necklace was wrenched from her neck.

"No! Stop!" she yelled, waving frantically at the figure

running away at top speed. A man. Short but fast, his feet eating up the distance like a…cat.

Carch had taken off after him, but within seconds the man melted into the heavy foot traffic and vanished. She watched Carch halt and spin, searching desperately, then take off again until he, too, disappeared.

Seri stood peering after them, speechless with shock. Her fingers sought her empty neck. How could this have happened?

And what should she do now?

Her cell phone rang and she hurried to answer it.

"Go back to Tildy's. Now." Carch's command was clipped out between harsh breaths. She could hear him running, fast. "Wait there for me." Then the line went dead.

"Are you all right?"

The concerned inquiry jerked her back to her surroundings. A small clutch of passers-by had stopped and were now pressing in around her, offering to call the police and asking about her welfare.

"I'm fine," she responded with a false smile, suddenly aware that any one of them could be something other than they seemed. If there were two assassins working together… My God, this could be a trap! "Really," she assured them, backing away. "Thanks, but I'll call the police from home."

She turned and started hurrying back to Queen Street. But she took the long way around in order to stick to the main thoroughfares. If something happened, she wanted plenty of witnesses.

When she finally made it to the courtyard, out of breath and barely holding it together, Carch was waiting for her on the bench. In a movement, he rose and strode toward her. He seemed…taller than usual.

For a split second she wondered if it was really him.

But as soon as he took her in his arms and murmured, "Thank God," she knew without a doubt he was her lover. The tingle of his otherworld presence rushed over her skin and she nestled deep into his strong, secure embrace. The familiar scent of him soothed her frazzled nerves as nothing else could.

"I couldn't catch the bastard," he said, his voice tight with frustration. "He kept changing forms on me. The only way I could follow was by sensing the residual energy of the shifts. But I lost him in the Market."

The Market was a long, open-air series of stalls selling everything under the sun, reminiscent of the French Market in New Orleans. It had been in the same place for hundreds of years and was always packed shoulder-to-shoulder with souvenir and bargain hunters. She could easily see how the thief could elude capture there.

"So now what do we do?" she asked worriedly.

"Go home and regroup."

"You really think your place is safe?"

He didn't answer right away. She glanced up at his face. It reflected more concern than she'd ever seen there before. "I don't know," he finally admitted. "The traitor will be angry once he realizes the necklace he took is not the real one."

"He'll be able to tell?"

For a second, the concern in Carch's face morphed to indecision. Then he sighed, and said, "The real one has powers that any Galifracian will be able to feel."

"What kind of powers?" she asked. When he'd told her about the necklace, he'd mentioned it being special, and something about a ceremony involved with it. But he hadn't gotten specific, and she hadn't asked.

"To an empath, wearing it greatly widens the extent of one's abilities. You can sense not only what others around you are thinking, but also get an impression of their past and future. In the royal ceremony held every fifty-two years, it is used to auger the future of the king and thereby the planet's welfare during the coming years. And it helps to choose his successor."

Somewhere during the explanation, her mouth had dropped open. As a scientist, she found what he said impossible to believe. But then, nearly everything of the past two days had been impossible to believe.

"It can really do those things?"

He nodded and took her hand to walk through the passageway and out to the street. "It can."

Good lord. No wonder losing it was considered treason. What had Derrik been thinking, giving such a valuable object to her aunt, even if it was to safeguard it from his enemies?

Carch paused looking both ways, seemingly undecided.

"Where should we go?" she asked.

"Maybe we should check into a hotel?"

All at once she had a terrible thought. "What about Aunt Tildy?"

He let out an oath, then pulled out his cell phone and dialed 411. "The *Post and Courier,*" he clipped out. When he was connected, he asked for John Grodin. She frowned. But before she could ask what he was doing, he was talking to the man on the other end. After a short, pointed conversation, he hung up. "Grodin's headed over here. He'll stay with Tildy for now."

She stared at him. "So you don't think Grodin's the traitor?"

"I used the phone company to connect the call, not the number on his card. I figure if he answers at the newspaper, we can probably trust him. At least that he's human," he amended as they started walking.

She followed his logic, and for now was reassured that her aunt would be safe. During their first meeting, she'd suspected the reporter had a bit of a crush on "Miss Tildy," so she hoped he'd go out of his way to play up his macho side to impress her.

Assuming he really wasn't an alien.

A few blocks later Carch paused in front of a small, out-of-the-way hotel. "What do you think? Should we play it safe?"

She looked up at the chicly shabby brass sign and vine-covered entrance. It looked perfect. But suddenly she was swamped by a feeling of wrongness, of urgency. All her instincts went on red alert.

She put her hand over her mouth and wanted to laugh, but couldn't choke past the irony. Ever since her parents had died, she'd relied on cool, controlled logic and observation to make her decisions. To keep her safe from the pain and hardships of emotions. Since when did she get "swamped" by any kind of feelings?

Since she'd met Carch Sunstryker, that's when. Since he had turned her entire life upside down. Since he'd made her realize she would never be, could never be safe from feelings. And the only thing to do was jump in with both feet.

"No." She took a deep breath and shook her head. "The bank's open for another forty-five minutes," she said. "I think we should get that necklace right now."

Chapter 16

"Back so soon?" The lady who had helped Carch and Seri this morning gave him a wide smile of recognition as he made his request to open the safety deposit box again.

In response he held up a manila envelope he'd filled with blank pieces of paper. "May as well get it all tucked away today, safe and sound, eh?" He hadn't dared alter his appearance, figuring she'd remember his name. A mistake he'd been too distracted to think of this morning.

"Absolutely," she said, reaching for her keys and rising from her desk. "A very good idea. So often people rent a box but never get around to putting their valuables into it."

"Pretty strange," he remarked, resisting the urge to check his watch again. Seri was outside biding her time to play her part in the new plan. They had a down-to-the-second timetable for their attempt on box 473, but checking his watch too often would be a sure red flag for any halfway-alert bank official.

And unnecessary. So far everything had gone exactly according to schedule.

He followed her into the vault, prepared to spend a few minutes retrieving and organizing their own box. Then at the exact same moment both his and Seri's cell phones would vibrate in their pockets, triggering the planned attack.

He waited calmly. He'd be more exposed without Seri in the room to help cover his actions, but he was actually very glad she wasn't. If the worst happened, he would eventually find a way to escape jail by shapeshifting. But she'd be stuck. And she'd have a record. Which would affect her life permanently—at least on Earth….

Of course, if he had his way she wouldn't be staying on Earth. She'd be coming with him. Seeing her wearing the Imperial Star had triggered something within him. A visceral knowledge that this was the woman he belonged with. He'd made up his mind. Now it was only a matter of convincing her. Somehow.

The furious vibrating of his cell phone in his pocket snapped him back to the present. He sauntered into position, slowly counting to ten. That would give her enough time to drop the bags filled with glass florist's marbles he'd bought at the flower shop up the street. They wouldn't command the excitement a jar full of money would, but it was the best they could come up with on short notice. They didn't have time to go back to Tildy's.

Even in the vault, he heard when the deluge of glass hit the stone-tile floor of the lobby. It sounded like a thousand guns going off at once. If that didn't distract everyone within hearing distance, nothing would.

Immediately he sprang into action, inserting his lock picks into the keyholes of box 473 and focusing all his concentration on springing the lock. It took him about fifteen seconds o open it. An eternity, it seemed. All he could do was pray no one was watching as he whisked the door open and yanked out the box.

He flipped the lid up, revealing the contents: a single packet of photographs. Nothing else.

Devils of Taron.

The necklace was not there!

Chapter 17

"What do you *mean* it wasn't there?"

Seri's cheeks were still bright red from the bank ordeal, but Carch didn't know whether from the exertion of picking up seven hundred glass marbles off the floor, or from pure embarrassment. But at his news her cheeks went pale as a Neshellon snowfall, and *that*, he figured, was from dismay.

"The only thing in box 473 was a packet of photos similar to the one we saw of the Imperial Star at the Thin Man Gallery," he said. "All sorts of jewelry and artifacts. Posed. Like for a catalogue or something."

Seri jammed the canvas money sack a bank employee had loaned her for the marbles into his arms and let out a low groan, pressing her temples with her fingers. "You have *got* to be kidding!"

"Believe me, I wish I were." He adjusted the bag, barely containing the anger and frustration that threatened to over whelm him. "Looks like we're back to square one." He adjusted the awkward bag again.

"Can we please get *rid* of those damn marbles?" she said between clenched teeth.

The flower shop where they'd bought them not half an hour ago was just a few doors down. After depositing the bag on the counter and saying, "Thanks, but we changed our minds," they left the florist gaping after them and continued walking. To where, he had no idea.

"I think I need a drink," Carch said.

He had been so certain the Imperial Star would be in box 473. Like a fool, he hadn't even considered alternatives. How irresponsible could he be? All this time they should have been—

What? What could he have been doing? Knowing who stole the necklace didn't make getting it back any easier. It just narrowed the field a bit.

"I'm sure we didn't miss any hiding place when we searched the gallery," Seri said when they'd found a small pub, ordered beers and slid into a secluded booth in the back.

He gazed at her worried face and was filled with wonder. She had taken up his cause as her own, as though it were *her* family's safety that depended upon the outcome.

He had never met a woman like her before. Loyal, passionate, selfless, intelligent. A woman worthy of being his companion as well as his lover. How could he ever have doubted his decision?

But if he lost her because of this insane—

"Carch?"

He realized she was peering at him with a puzzled look on her face. *Damn.* How many times had she said his name?

"Do you?"

"I'm sorry. What?" He must keep his mind on his task! Or

he would lose everything. Everything in his past, as well as everything he might have in his future.

"Do you think we should search the gallery again?"

He gave his head a shake, as much to rid himself of his disheartening thoughts as in answer. "No, I agree with you. We didn't miss anything. It must be somewhere else."

"David and Alan's home, maybe?"

"Possibly." He took a long draught of beer and pondered for a moment. "Detective Williams said they were under investigation for bigger things than one necklace."

"Yeah," she agreed slowly. "So?"

"So, where are all the records? We didn't find anything at the gallery that didn't seem totally legal. And if they're that careful, I'm guessing there is nothing at their home, either."

She nodded, catching on to the direction of his thoughts. "Which means they must have some other place where they keep their records and stolen goods."

"Exactly." He pressed his lips together.

"So if we find that place—"

"With any luck, we'll find the Imperial Star, too."

Carch and Seri decided to stay and have supper at the pub, then walk over to the Second Sun to check on Tildy before doing anything else.

They found her sitting with John Grodin in the parlor having after-dinner tea. They didn't dare fill her in on what had happened at the bank. It would wait. They stayed for a cup, anyway, and while passing the sugar Carch took the opportunity to probe Grodin subtly for any useful information.

Seri was right. The reporter did have a little crush on "Miss Tildy." But those were about the only feelings his mind revealed. Nothing about the Imperial Star; nothing about the owners of the Thin Man Gallery. Carch didn't sense the man shielding anything from him, he just wasn't thinking about anything except having tea with Tildy.

When they rose to go, Tildy urged Grodin to take his leave, as well.

"I'm perfectly safe here on my own," she insisted. "I appreciate your company, but this is really all just nonsense. I don't own anything else anyone would possibly want to steal." Which had been their excuse for getting Grodin over there in the first place. A tie-in to his article.

And without telling Grodin and Tildy the full extent of their reasons, Carch and Seri's concern did indeed look a bit inflated.

"Even so, I don't mind staying, Miss Tildy, honest," Grodin said with a smile that made Tildy's freeze in place. Poor old thing. She obviously didn't return her bodyguard's tender regard.

Carch once again thought of the envelope he had at home for her from his grandfather. She'd been only twenty years old when she'd met Derrik, and yet in all these years she had not met a man who had taken his place in her affections. Did she still love him?

Carch's gaze slid to Seri, who was again watching him expectantly. He, for one, was not going to force another man on Tildy if she didn't want him around. And she was probably right about being safe. The traitor knew she hadn't recovered the necklace. Carch's fears for her safety had been born from the anxiety of the moment, not any real danger that he could see now that he was thinking rationally.

"I'd hate to inconvenience you any further," he told Grodin. "Perhaps you could ask your police contacts to step up patrols through the courtyard tonight," he suggested as a compromise.

Grodin's face fell in disappointment. Tildy looked relieved. Seri still had a worried frown.

"I s'pose I could do that," Grodin said. "If you're sure she'll be okay."

"Promise you'll call if you hear anything strange, or are in the least bit nervous," Seri urged her aunt.

"I will, sweetheart."

That settled, they made sure she locked all her doors, and then they headed for the street.

"So, hotel or home?" he asked Seri.

"Home," she said, taking his hand with a smile. He smiled back, kissed her, and they started the mile or so walk to the house.

Summer days in Charleston he found uncomfortably hot and humid, but he loved the nights. The warm, sultry air was filled with the fragrance of a million flowers blossoming in the small, lush gardens Charlestonians loved so well. Music drifted out from the many fine restaurants and other establishments tucked into the historic rows of buildings they passed, and a light sea breeze floated in from the bay as they strolled along under a black night sky spangled with a billion glittering stars.

Many of which Carch had visited. But with the sole exception of Galifrax, none felt as…right…as here on Earth. Was it because of his mother? Or was it because of the woman walking next to him?

"Tired of walking?" he asked Seri, wrapping his arm around her shoulders. They'd been on their feet all day. Like a tiny version of Manhattan—and in marked contrast to his home of Eldor—on the Charleston Peninsula most people walked to the places they frequented in their daily lives. The compact town was their whole world, and anything off peninsula didn't count. Carch had grown to like walking everywhere. But he didn't know what she was used to in Phoenix.

"Are you kidding? I'm a teacher. I walk miles every day in the classroom."

He chuckled. "True. I guess I usually do, too, come to think of it. The sci-cruisers I travel around on are pretty huge."

Her eyes sparked with interest. "Yeah? How huge?"

"About the size of a football stadium. One of the big ones." He grinned at her dropped jaw. "It has to be big, carrying several hundred people for light years at a time."

"Then how did it land on Earth without being seen, or detected?"

"The actual ship remains in orbit and a smaller transport ship is sent to the surface. Its outside is shielded so it's pretty hard to detect by your radar."

She asked him even more questions, and he told her about the various spacecraft he'd flown on and how they worked, about the planets he'd visited and the people and creatures that inhabited them.

But the more he talked, the quieter she became.

Damn.

He should have known answering her questions would be a mistake. Instead of bringing them closer, the conversation was driving them further apart. It drove home as nothing else could that he was leaving.

"What about you?" he asked, wanting to draw her out again. Back to him. "Do you like being a teacher?"

She glanced up, smiling. "Yes. I do. I know some teachers think it's frustrating work because it's so hard to reach kids nowadays. My philosophy is that every child I am able to turn on to the wonders of science is a victory. Their lives might not be changed by it, but I hope they're a bit richer for understanding the world around them."

"You like working with kids," he said. That knowledge had permeated every word of her answer.

He had steered their path home via the Battery, the long curving boardwalk atop a storm wall that protected the low-lying city from the temper of the sea. He liked coming here at night to gaze out over the bay, watching the lights of the boats coming and going and the stars slowly rotating overhead, just as he did from his balcony back home.

They climbed the steps to the top of the wall and she gazed out over the water. Although his remark hadn't really been a question, she said, "Yes. I like kids a lot."

Did he detect a note of wistfulness in her voice?

"You want children of your own?" he asked. She was only thirty or so, too young to have given up on having them, which might have explained the wistfulness.

She sighed. "I've decided not to have children," she said, surprising him with her forthrightness. And with the statement itself.

"Why?"

"That would involve having a man," she said simply.

He turned to her in wary confusion. He knew with the certainty of hours spent in her bed that she liked men. Sex couldn't be the problem. "What does that mean?"

Again she sighed, this time longer and deeper. "All my life I've been surrounded by women whose men have deserted them. I'd just as soon skip that whole ordeal."

So there it was out in the open. The reason for that awful fear of abandonment he'd sensed the first time they'd made love.

Like an exploding star, a deep understanding blazed through him. Of her answer about children, but also of her stubborn refusal to take their relationship any further.

He'd felt from the beginning her profound fear of becoming involved on any level, but now he understood it was the limitations he himself had put on that relationship that kept her from opening up.

She was terrified she would give up everything to be with him, only to have him desert her when they arrived on an alien planet.

One thing was painfully clear.

She would never be his mistress. She wanted more. She

wanted a permanent commitment, like the one his parents had. Nothing else would do.

Good God. No wonder she hadn't taken him seriously.

"What would you do," he asked, very careful to keep his tone neutral, "if you found you were pregnant?"

Her gaze snapped to his, eyes wide. "By you?"

"Yes."

"You said I couldn't be." Her expression was suddenly furious and accusing.

"I said you *wouldn't* be. The chances are negligible. It took seven years for my mother to conceive. But I am living proof it does, occasionally, rarely, happen."

Her mouth parted as his words sank in. "You *lied* to me?"

"I wanted you. So I took a calculated risk." He jetted out a breath. "Angel, if someone had told you a week ago that there was a risk you might be sleeping with an extraterrestrial today, would you have given the idea any credence whatsoever?"

She stared at him, pressing her lips into a thin line.

Point to the spaceman.

"There's such a thing as protection," she ground out.

"Your kind of protection doesn't work for me. The whole shapeshifter thing."

"My God," she muttered.

"Would it be so bad?" he asked sincerely.

She squeezed her eyes shut. "To be impregnated by an alien?"

He tried to decide whether or not to be offended. Logic told him no, but his heart…another matter.

"No," he said. "To have a child with the man you love."

"I don't love you," she denied, but wouldn't look at him. "I can't love a man from another planet. A man who, in the best case will be leaving in two days without me, and in the worst may be dead any minute."

He saw her dilemma. He did. But that didn't mean he

accepted her answer to it, even if right now he couldn't tell her what she needed to hear.

"You do love me," he refuted. He enfolded her in his embrace, forcing her to open her eyes and see him. Then he kissed her.

She hesitated for a heartbeat, then sank into his arms and opened to him, even while whispering, "No. I really don't."

He lifted from the kiss with a sense of profound longing. "Come back with me," he said, unable to stop himself. "Let me prove how wrong you are." *About everything. About your fears. About your love. About mine.* "I'll be good to you, Seri. So good."

"I'm sorry, Carch, I can't."

And yet he could feel her thinking. About Galifrax. About him. About the vast differences between them on nearly every level. About the unlikelihood of them as a couple.

But he also sensed that wasn't the real problem. She knew it didn't matter what planet you came from, what shape your eyes were, or the color of your hair and skin. What mattered was inside. What mattered were your feelings for each other. And she did not trust his.

Admittedly, he had come to Earth with a mind full of pre-judices and preconceived ideas about the women here. But Seri had crashed every one of them. Or rather, she had lived up to every one of them, but at the same time had taught him the wonderful value of her stubbornness, her inquisitiveness, intelligence and logic, her independence and outspokenness. Her loyalty meant all the more because of them.

He wanted her. He wanted her to be his. His alone.

But the ultimate irony was, those traits he had come to admire so much were the very things that kept her from surrendering to what they both wanted. She only trusted what her head told her. Not her heart.

The problem was, her head was right. He'd given her no reason to trust her heart. He'd offered her no promises, no binding commitment, no reason to believe he wouldn't desert her as those other men had deserted her, her mother and her aunt. But he couldn't do that. Not yet.

As he gazed down into her clear green eyes, he knew he'd be a bastard if he promised her more without being absolutely certain he could keep those promises. As she'd pointed out, he might be dead any minute. And if he failed in his mission…

If he made her those promises, and something happened to him, if they didn't end up together, it would be far worse for her to spend the rest of her life thinking of the years they might have had together, rather than thinking he'd just used her. If she thought that, she could move on when he was gone, find someone else. Live a full life without him. As much as the thought pained him to the core, he knew it was the right thing to do.

Tonight, the only thing he could offer her with any honor was the potent sexual chemistry they shared. He cupped her face in his hand. "I understand," he forced himself to say. "But then come to bed with me now. You promised me that, at least."

Chapter 18

On the sidewalk outside Carch's grand house, Seri banked the aching emotions brought to the surface by their conversation, and glanced around nervously.

Last time they'd walked up this path Carch had been shot and nearly died.

Was the assassin somewhere out there even now, watching, waiting for another chance? Regardless of her chaotic feelings about the man who was breaking her heart, she couldn't bear it if something terrible happened to him.

"Don't worry," he said. "The traitor won't kill me yet. He knows we're getting close to the real necklace. He'll wait until we have it, then close in. He showed his strategy this afternoon when he stole the fake one."

"You really think so?" she asked. Hoping he was right, but not quite believing it.

"Sure I do," Carch said, planting a kiss on her forehead and handing her the key. "But just in case, you go first. I'll wait here in plain view until you're safely inside."

So much for him believing it, either. She pushed the key back in his hand. "Forget it." Did he really expect her to leave him standing there like a target? "You're coming with me." She put her arm around his waist and started running for the house.

Left with no choice, he ran with her, unlocked the door in a flash and they tumbled into the foyer.

"Are you *crazy?*" he burst out after he'd slammed the door and locked it again. He grabbed her and pulled her to his chest. She could feel his heart beating like a tympani. "Don't you *ever* take a chance like that again!"

"I knew you were lying."

"I wasn't. I just don't want—" He broke off with a growl, compelled her chin up and kissed her hard. "Dammit, Seri." He kissed her again with almost bruising intensity. "When will you learn to obey me?"

He started backing her toward the staircase, kissing her all the way; when she stumbled he caught her up in his strong arms, then took the stairs two at a time up to his room.

The rest of the world—his imminent departure, her aching heart, the necklace, the traitor—everything fell away as he laid her on his bed and lowered himself over her. He slipped an arm under her neck and pulled her hard against him. A shimmering avalanche of potent energy buried them deep in its powerful grip.

"In this, at least, you obey me."

"Yes," she whispered.

She gave herself up completely to it, to his will, drugged with desire, unable to resist him even if she wanted to. Her mouth sought his, her lips telling him of her infinite need. He tasted so good, so exotic and exciting, so like nothing else she'd ever tasted. She couldn't get enough of him.

"Carch," she moaned, drilling her fingers into his hair to pull him closer, wanting more. She felt his need, his desire, as her own.

An answering groan vibrated in his throat and he reached for her shirt front, impatiently ripping it open. Buttons flew. She gasped. He slid down to claim her breasts with both hands, cupping them, holding them firmly as he drew one, then the other into his mouth. Rough ribbons of need spiraled through her as he used his teeth and tongue to suckle her deeply. She cried out with the sweet pleasure-pain of it.

He reached for her skirt, made quick work of the zipper and tugged feverishly at her remaining clothes until she was naked under him.

"You, too," she pleaded, needing to feel his bare skin and his hard male body against her. "The real you."

He gazed down at her for a split second, then nodded, stripped off his clothes and came back to her in a fluid series of moves. Then he gripped her hips and buried his face in her belly. A shivering, tingling sensation flowed over her and a moment later a long shudder passed through him. The air around them lit up with a golden glow.

Rejoicing at his trust, she bathed her senses in his sensual glamour and the warm, trembling vibrations with which it caressed her skin, in the sound of his low groans as he touched her body. And in the spicy, musky scent of his desire for her.

He looked up and she realized he had changed all the way. His exotic slanted eyes gazed at her with a heat that melted her completely. She slid her fingers through his flowing golden hair then drew them slowly over his striking, chiseled features. He was so different, but so very handsome.

"Do you still want me?" he asked, his beautiful eyes momentarily uncertain.

"More than anything," she assured him.

It was the truth, she realized. She wanted him more than her familiar life, more than her known world. More than her need for control. He meant more to her than anything.

"I want to taste you," he murmured, and returned his mouth to her belly, settling his shoulders into the cradle of her thighs. His powerful hands compelled her knees wide apart.

He moved yet farther down and his tongue licked over the center of her desire. She cried out, arching her whole body at the explosion of pleasure. He made love to her there, assiduously and expertly, his tongue tracing taut circles around her small bud of thrilling need. She gulped down ragged gasps as he relentlessly pushed her to the brink of oblivion.

"Oh! *Carch.*"

Blinding pleasure claimed her body, racking it again and again as a brilliant climax ripped through her. And then he did it again.

She sobbed out his name when, finally, his scorching body came up hard on her, covering her like a blanket of fire, taking her last breath as he entered her with a single forceful stroke.

She screamed. Between her legs there was an unfamiliar, blindingly erotic sensation. He felt different…*felt better.* A thousand times more pleasurable!

"Wh-what…is…i-it?" she stammered between gulps of air.

"The real me. I told you there were…differences."

She'd almost forgotten. Holding herself still, she tried to feel what they might be. She felt filled to the hilt. More than filled. Inside her, he felt huge and heavy like carved stone, and long and slick like oil on glass, and yet…fluid and undulating. Like something that really should need batteries.

She felt lightheaded with excitement. *Oh, my—*

He flexed his hips and a solid ripple moved from the root of his amazing sex to the tip and back again. His hands were still gripping her firmly under her knees, holding her thighs wide apart. She grabbed his biceps, trying to clamp her legs together against the almost frighteningly incredible sensation. He forced them farther up and out.

She let out a whimper.

"Don't be scared," he said, his voice low and rough with restraint. "It can't hurt you. It conforms to your shape. And I can feel what you enjoy, remember?"

She sucked in a breath. At the moment she couldn't remember her own name.

"Trust me. Let yourself go, my angel."

She nodded, and with a shiver of fear—and a thrill of anticipation—she surrendered her control to him.

Her pulse beat so hard she could feel it throb around that part of him deep inside her. An answering throb emanated from him there, slowly building up in intensity until it became a hard, undulating wave of pleasure moving all along his length.

She moaned, arching under him.

"Good?" he whispered.

"More," she moaned mindlessly.

He obliged her. And her whole being came apart as a dazzling orgasm tore through her without warning.

A masculine grunt of satisfaction sounded in his throat.

"Don't stop," she moaned, and he began to ride her, thrusting himself deep into her and pulling out again in a primitive, savage rhythm. Her body arched and bucked with pleasure, all pretense of control decimated. She was helpless to do anything but accept the onslaught of his deep, hard ecstasy.

His thick, heavy arousal scythed in and out, showing no mercy, driving her to another tumultuous climax. Finally, when she was sure there was not a scintilla of sensation left that he had not wrung from her, he arched his back, reared up and roared out his release.

* * *

Seri clung to him, her body stunned and trembling with repletion…and emotion.

She had never given herself to another human being so thoroughly, so completely, so utterly that there was no going back.

Did Carch realize what had just happened to her? Had he sensed it in her mind or in her body? Or did he think this had simply been another round of "ordinary sex"?

Was this ordinary on his planet?

The mind boggled.

He held her close, supporting his weight above her with his forearms as they both caught their breath. After several minutes she felt him watching her.

She cracked her eyelids and dared a look at him. Sure enough, he was peering down at her, a tiny frown between his brows, as though he could feel the inner turmoil roiling within her. Or was it something else?

"What are you shielding from me?" he quietly asked.

"Nothing," she lied.

"Don't lie to me. What are you hiding, Seri? Didn't I…?" He let out a soft curse. "My form…didn't please you." With the words he closed his eyes and before she could stop him a shudder passed through him, and suddenly she was gazing into his human eyes, crystal-blue and filled with regret.

She shook her head. "No. I mean, yes! You pleased me, Carch. Every part of you. So very much." At his doubtful look, she added softly, "So much it scares me."

"Why would pleasure scare you?" He seemed genuinely puzzled. But she wasn't about to enlighten him. Loving him was not a confession she was ready to make. She buried the thought.

"Because I fear it may prove addictive," she said with a bleak smile.

"But that's a good thing." He kissed her tenderly, and

winked. "It will help pass the time on the long voyage back to Galifrax."

She licked her lips. Tasted him. "Carch—"

He put his fingers to her mouth. "Shhh. You are coming with me. I'll hear no argument."

She wasn't going to argue. The truth was, she'd made up her mind. If he honestly wanted her to go with him, she would. Even at the risk of ending up alone and abandoned on a strange planet. But…he had to give her a reason to believe.

"Carch—"

"I love your stubbornness," he said, shocking her into silence with the first three unexpected words. "But let's talk about this tomorrow," he went on, thankfully not noticing the blinding hope that had bounded into her eyes only to be blinked back again. "We both desperately need sleep. Let's get it while we can."

She nodded, easing out a long breath. She couldn't have talked anyway, not if her life had depended on it.

She was a fool. Foolish, foolish girl. She might have fallen head over heels for him, but he was a prince, a commanding, worldly man who could have any woman he chose. Right now, he claimed to want her. But later, after months, or years if she was lucky, would he still feel the same way?

Could he ever learn to love her?

And if he didn't, would the memory of loving him, of being with him for whatever time he gave her, would those memories be enough to sustain her in a strange new place after he abandoned her? Would those precious extra days or months be worth the hurt of losing both him and everything she knew?

If only he would say he loved her! Then she could be sure. Then she could take the risk and make the decision she so longed to make, and give herself the chance to be his, forever.

Chapter 19

"Why don't we just make them an offer for it?"

Carch gazed uncomprehendingly at Seri. "Huh? An offer?"

It was the next morning and they'd been lying in bed discussing what their next move would be to find the Imperial Star. Time was getting distressingly short. There were less than thirty-six hours before the scheduled sci-cruiser transport arrived to take him back to Galifrax. If he didn't have it by then—

"Yeah," she said, plumping the pillow she'd propped her arms and chin on. She looked so delectable lying there sprawled across his bed, all rumpled by his lovemaking and so sexy and desirable he lost his train of thought.

"You offered the pawn shops a ten-thousand-dollar reward," she went on, pulling his focus back up to her eyes. "Why don't you offer the same to David and Alan?"

He tried to concentrate, but was having trouble remembering what she was talking about. "For what?"

"The necklace, of course!"

His mouth dropped open. Okay. An offer. On the necklace? "But…that's nuts."

"Why? Who knows how much they expected to make from selling it on the black market? And with cops hanging around the courtyard curtailing business, maybe they'll take the easy money if you offer it. Ten grand is a pretty good chunk of change."

He stared at her, finally getting it. *Devils of Taron!* Why the *hell* hadn't he thought of that?

He gave a bark of laughter. *Pure genius.* "My God." He dove onto the bed and rolled her into a big kiss, then pulled away to regard her with no small dose of admiration. "Anyone ever tell you how amazing you are?"

Her cheeks turned bright red, but she looked pleased. "Not lately."

He gave her another kiss. "Well, you are. Completely, utterly amazing." He rolled off the bed again, giving her bare bottom a smack. "Get dressed. We have a necklace to buy!"

"I've no idea what you're talking about."

David Brash was a stylish, fiftyish man with a salt-and-pepper beard and sharp, intelligent eyes. His partner Alan Richards was thinner and balding, but his clothes were cutting edge. They presented a pleasantly smiling—and determinedly ignorant—united front.

"We know you have Tildy Woodson's necklace," Carch said implacably. He'd added a couple of inches to his usual height so he really loomed over them as he spoke, but the subtle intimidation was having little visible effect. These guys had innocence down to an art.

"We are not interested in how you obtained it," Seri said. "We simply want it back."

"As I said, we have no idea to what you are referring—"

Obviously a different strategy was needed. Carch pulled out one of the thick packets of cash—all hundreds—he'd stowed in his inner jacket pocket and held it up. That got the duo's attention.

They looked at the money, then David narrowed his eyes. "Okaaay. Not saying we have, but suppose we had seen this mythical necklace? What are we talking?"

"I'm holding ten thousand dollars. You hand me the necklace, I hand you the cash. No questions asked."

Alan's astonished gaze hadn't left the packet. But now they darted to the window and the courtyard, then back to him. His pointed chin went up and he huffed dramatically. "You're a cop. Or a fed. This is your feeble attempt at entrapment."

Carch opened his mouth, but Seri spoke before he had a chance. "We made you the offer, not the other way around, so it's not entrapment. In fact, it proves we're not cops. Remember, there's no crime in giving you a reward for finding something my aunt carelessly lost."

The four of them studied each other in silence for several moments.

"True," David said at length. He and Alan exchanged glances. "We did find it in the courtyard and were wondering who it belonged to."

"Now you know. And we are very grateful you kept it safe."

"You're welcome." Alan smiled, twirled his fingers and cocked a hip. "But I'm afraid ten thousand isn't enough."

Carch pushed out a breath of disgust. "Yeah. I had a feeling that might be the case." Which was why he'd brought a lot more than ten grand with him. He pulled out another packet. "Here's another ten. My final offer." It wasn't, but no sense telling them he'd pay any amount for the necklace.

The money meant nothing to Carch. When he'd landed on

Earth, the only thing he'd brought with him was a bag filled
with precious gems from Galifrax, carefully selected for their
compatibility with types from Earth. Those were quickly exchanged for cash.

Every time he came to a planet where money was still in
use, he was glad Galifrax had moved beyond the archaic
system of personal wealth. This was one of the lesser
examples of the greed money produced, but it was no less re-
pellent for that. Carch could see it ooze over both the other
men's faces. David stretched out his hand to take the packets
of money from him.

Carch flicked them out of reach. "When I get the necklace,
you get the cash," he reminded them tersely.

"But—"

"Not negotiable. Now, go fetch it."

"But we can't," Alan rushed to say with a nasal whine.

"We put it somewhere very safe," David explained. "It'll
take some time to retrieve it."

Alan's eyes darted worriedly to the packets of money as
Carch stabbed them back into his pocket.

"How long will it take?" he demanded.

Where the hell had they stashed the necklace? It was a
damned good thing Seri had suggested doing this. Otherwise
he had the sinking feeling he'd never have found it before his
time was up. Obviously these two thieves were not the op-
portunistic amateurs he'd originally thought. They were
seasoned pros.

"We can have it here by tomorrow," David said.

Tomorrow?

Damn it! That was cutting things far too close for comfort.
The transport ship would land after dark tomorrow night, expecting to scoop up Carch and take off again before being
detected. If there was any delay getting the Imperial Star, he

would have to invent a credible reason for staying longer—a dangerous prospect. Yes, the ship was shielded against visual detection, but the longer it hung around, the more likely the void created on the radar by the orbiting sci-cruiser would be mathematically detected and traced—by the military, a university researcher, NASA, some crackpot UFO watcher. He cringed just thinking about the possibilities.

"Nine in the morning," he told them firmly. "After that, the deal's off."

"But—"

"We'll meet you here at nine. Understand?"

Both men nodded, although it was clear they didn't like the ultimatum. Well, too bad. Carch didn't like it either. He just prayed they'd come through in the morning. If they didn't, things would get ugly.

He and Seri went out the gallery's back door into the courtyard.

"Do you trust them?" she asked worriedly.

He jetted out a curse. "Do we have a choice?"

Just then Madam Clarissa appeared at the door to her shop, giving them the evil eye before calling out to her damned cats. He noticed Seri watched warily as the big black tom that had given her such a scare the other night ambled by, also giving them a gimlet eye.

"I *still* think that beast looks suspicious," Seri muttered under her breath. "Do Galifracians by any chance have a special fondness for fish?"

Though he wasn't at all certain she was wrong about the cat, he chuckled. "Not so's you'd notice. But don't worry," he assured her straight-faced. "If it comes to a fight, I can take it, no problem."

That teased a laugh out of her. He was glad. Her smiles were getting rarer and rarer. He hated that. Because he was the reason she'd stopped smiling. She was obviously worried about his fate. But it was more than that. He knew she was struggling with the fate of their relationship, as well. Struggling with whether she'd come with him. It was an either or proposition, all or nothing, whichever answer she chose, irrevocable. And he hadn't made it any easier on her by keeping mute about the full extent of his feelings for her. He was almost relieved he wasn't in a position to have to make that decision himself.

Except he wanted her so badly he'd do almost anything to have her, to make her come home with him. Home to Galifrax. It was killing him that she didn't trust him. For him it was a no-brainer.

Unfortunately, he wasn't the one who got to choose.

"Shall we go check on Aunt Tildy?" Seri asked.

"Sure." In addition to the cash, he carried something else in his pocket. The envelope for Tildy from his grandfather. No time like the present to give it to her.

Suddenly, a low, accusing masculine voice sounded from the passageway. "What were you two doing at the Thin Man Gallery?"

Carch turned to see Detective Williams, still dressed as a bum, standing with his hands on his grubby hips scowling at them.

"Nothing that concerns you," Carch answered levelly.

"And I suppose that wasn't bundles of cash you offered those two felons?" Williams asked, eyes slitted suspiciously.

"Why? Is it illegal to pay by cash now?"

"To buy stolen goods, it is."

Carch was getting annoyed with the direction of this conversation. "As it happens, I didn't buy anything."

"Believe me, Detective Williams," Seri interjected, "all we're interested in is finding my aunt's missing necklace.

Carch was just telling the owners of the Thin Man about the reward he's offering for its recovery."

Williams shifted, pinning Carch with a challenging glare. "Looked like a lot of money."

But it was Seri who answered. "It's a valuable necklace. Not to mention the purely sentimental value. My aunt is devastated by its loss."

"A lot of money for the owner of a bookstore I have yet to see a customer go into," Williams continued as though she hadn't spoken, still glaring at him. "Care to explain that, Mr. Sunstryker?"

Inwardly Carch swore an oath. This was exactly what he'd feared might happen. That if this cop hung around long enough, he'd start shining the spotlight on him.

"The bookstore is my hobby, not my income," Carch said. "My family has money, Detective Williams. Lots of it." And that was the gods' honest truth. Not that he thought for a minute the cop would take his word for it. And when his background check didn't find a rich family, or even a record of his own existence…

"Just remember," Williams said, leaning into his face. "I'm watching you."

For a split second, a tension arced so powerfully between them that it raised the hairs on his arms. The guy was definitely wound too tight. Or was it…something else Carch sensed? Something more…personal?

"Watch all you like," he said calmly, then took Seri's arm and walked away.

Whatever it was he'd felt, the man was trouble. Carch could only hope that before the cop dug too deep on him and got really suspicious, he'd have the necklace and be gone for good.

Seri put her arm around his waist and his heart lurched. But in another sense, he'd be gone all too soon. He looked down at her and suddenly the future was crystal-clear. In his heart he knew what he had to do or he'd regret it for the rest of his life.

One way or another, willingly or no, Serenity June Woodson was coming with him.

Chapter 20

The Second Sun Crystal and Tarot Salon was open for business. Through the windows Seri could see several customers roaming among the cozily cluttered aisles. She glanced at the bizarre row of buzzers lined up along the outside door frame as she and Carch approached the shop's entrance.

Press me if you're feeling blue…
Fame and fortune…
Revenge or protection…

Protection, she thought. Yep. Definitely, that should be her choice today, what she needed most.

But irrationally, it was the button that declared, Press me if you seek to find happiness and true love that drew her attention and just wouldn't let go.

Did she? Seek true love?

Or had she already found it? Why wouldn't he give her a sign? Or better yet, say the words she longed to hear?

She looked up at Carch and found him gazing down at her. She wondered if he could sense her thoughts. Or if they were so scary that she'd buried them too deep for him to detect.

"Which one would you choose today?" he asked, the ghost of a smile lifting his lips.

"Protection," she answered, hoping he wouldn't sense the lie.

He glanced away, gave a short nod, then turned back and kissed her on the forehead. "I'm going to check on the bookstore for a few minutes. Will you be okay alone?"

She made herself smile. "Of course."

But that was a lie, too. She wouldn't be okay alone—without him. Oh, for these few minutes today she'd be fine. But tomorrow night, when he left and she wasn't with him, no way would she be okay.

She loved him. As incredible as it sounded, she loved the damned spaceman. So very much.

But did he return her feelings? Wouldn't he have said something by now? Or was he waiting for her to say the words first?

Could she be bold enough to say them? *Should* she? Shouldn't she expect him to say he loved her without prompting? If he truly wanted her in the same way she wanted him, if he wanted her to come with him for all the right reasons and not for the wrong ones, surely he would let her know?

A customer walked out of the Second Sun, making the bell over the door tinkle in welcome. The scent of patchouli drifted over Seri, filling her with the comfort of a million memories and the steadfast love she'd always associated with it. She thought of all she'd be giving up if she chose to leave this world behind... And for what?

"Hello, Seri dear!" Aunt Tildy trilled from behind the sales counter. "What on earth are you doing standing outside? Come in! Come in!"

So, she resolutely fixed a bright smile on her face and went in.

Unfortunately, after giving her aunt a hug, the next person she saw was John Grodin. Probably paranoia—definitely paranoia—but she still didn't quite trust the man.

"Do you always put in this amount of time on your articles?" she asked after they exchanged greetings. "No wonder the price of newspapers is going up so much."

They both watched her aunt walk over to help a customer, then he gave Seri an enigmatic look. "I find the subject fascinating."

She hiked a brow. "And what subject would that be? My aunt? Tarot reading? The robbery?"

He shrugged, giving her a grin. "Guess you'll just have to buy the paper to find out." He glanced around the shop. "So, where's your boyfriend today?"

She didn't bother to correct him about the state of their relationship. "The bookstore. Carch does have a business to run."

"Ah, yes. Too bad. I thought he might be chasing down leads on the necklace."

"No such luck," she said, figuring that the reporter was fishing. She was not about to tip him off. Grodin sticking his nose in and spoiling the deal with David and Alan was all they'd need.

"Well, maybe I'll mosey on over to the Old World," he said. "I have a couple of questions I want to ask him." She looked up sharply and Grodin elaborated. "I did a quick search on all the shop owners in the courtyard. Background for the article. Interestingly, I struck out on Carch Sunstryker. Didn't find a single reference to him in any archive or database. Even the tax records came up empty. What do you think of that?"

She thought he ought to mind his own damned business. But saying so would no doubt just make him even more curious.

"Probably a pen name," she suggested, leaning in with a hushed, conspiratorial tone. "I'll bet he's a famous author who doesn't want his identity known, so he can be left in peace."

The reporter's eyes lit with curiosity. "Really?" He lowered his voice. "Who?"

"That would be telling," she whispered, then walked away, leaving him gaping after her.

With any luck he'd spend the next two days searching for pictures of every famous male author in the country, trying to figure out who Carch was. The thought almost made her chuckle as she walked up the apartment stairs to phone Carch and warn him.

Now if they could just get rid of Williams as easily.

Over the next hour or so, Seri helped her aunt with a spate of customers. It was just like old times. As a teen growing up under Aunt Tildy's care, she'd often helped in the shop. She was strictly a science girl herself, but she had to admit the kooky, slightly-south-of-normal people who frequented the Second Sun were a lot of fun. Eccentric. Open to the kind of phenomena that Seri had never believed in—until the day before yesterday.

She had never believed in a lot of things until the day before yesterday. UFOs. Extraterrestrials. Shapeshifters.

Love.

As in romantic love. Between a man and a woman.

And she still didn't. Because Carch didn't love her. Not truly. Her body, yes, he seemed to love that. But not her whole self.

But, oh! How she loved him. All of him. Every mysterious, glorious, wonderful inch of him. And that was the one thing she'd never believed possible, that she could let her precious guard down long enough to allow someone into her heart.

But she had. From the very first moment she'd seen him. One look at her golden god and she'd been a goner.

"Oh, dear," Aunt Tildy murmured sympathetically, pulling her out of her musings. Her aunt's expression was filled with concern as she peered at Seri. "I don't need my tarot cards to see that you and I should have a heart-to-heart."

The shop had emptied out, but Seri didn't particularly feel like baring her soul at the moment. Too many unresolved, chaotic feelings were running around inside her.

"There's really nothing to talk about."

"You are going with him, aren't you? Tomorrow, back to Galifrax," her aunt said with an oddly wistful look on her face.

"I don't think so," Seri said as evenly as possible.

"But why ever not? Hasn't he asked you?"

"Yes," she admitted.

"You don't believe he's serious?" Aunt Tildy asked somberly.

Seri sighed. "Oh, he's serious. Just not about me. Not in the way I need him to be in order to take the risk."

This was one love that was decidedly *not* written in the stars. Destiny? Possibly. But not the one she'd wished for.

She strove not to let the hurt show. But it did hurt. More than she could ever imagine. Or would acknowledge... Just because she was in love with the man didn't mean she had to wear her heart on her sleeve. Though, clearly something must be showing because her aunt had guessed her feelings so readily. Of course, her aunt *was* a psychic.

"Give him a chance. I'm sure he's just worried about the necklace," Aunt Tildy assured her, patting her hand.

"Maybe." Which reminded her of their good news. Thankful for a change of subject, she told her aunt about the deal with David and Alan. "Fingers crossed. The Imperial Star should be in our possession by morning."

Aunt Tildy beamed. "You see? I just knew Carch would

get it back. And don't worry, my love. Once it's in his hands, he'll tell you everything you want to hear. He loves you. I'm sure of it."

She wasn't about to burst her aunt's well-meaning bubble. She was so sweet. And obviously projecting, because she regretted not being able to fly away with Prince Derrik forty-two years ago.

Suddenly, Seri had a brilliant idea. "Why don't *you* go back with him?"

"Me?" Her aunt peered at her with surprise. And guilt, giving herself away.

Seri's jaw dropped. "You *have* been thinking about it, haven't you! Oh, Aunt Tildy, that's a wonderful idea! You must go with him!"

Her aunt's eyes lit softly. "Do you really think so?"

"Absolutely." Carch had mentioned that King Derrik had been a widower for many years now. And it was crystal clear that her aunt had never stopped loving him.

"It's been such a long time. What if Derrik doesn't feel the same way? What if he doesn't want me? After all, he sent his grandson back to Earth to retrieve the Imperial Star, not me."

Seri pulled her aunt into a warm hug. "Maybe he didn't dare hope or presume that you still loved him."

"If only I could know for certain."

"You should ask Carch."

Aunt Tildy gave a sigh. "I'm sure I'm just being a silly old woman with stars in her eyes. But maybe I will ask him. Tonight, at supper."

Seri gave her another hug. "Oh, Aunt Tildy, I just know everything will work out. You've always said your love for Derrik was written in those stars. It's about time you got to live your dreams."

She was so happy for her aunt. She was. She only wished

her own dreams would come true. But time was running out. And even if Carch pressed her to go with him, she still wasn't sure she could do it. She could live with being his mistress. But if he didn't love her… What kind of a future could she expect on a strange planet with a man who didn't love her?

Her heart squeezed painfully, tears suddenly burning her eyes. But then again, even in familiar surroundings, what kind of a future could she expect without the man she loved?

"I'm worried about that reporter," Carch announced when he returned to the Second Sun after finishing his business at the bookstore. He had been tying up loose ends from his month-long stay on Earth. He'd paid all the bills and given Abel Smalls, the manager, an envelope containing the legal paperwork transferring the deed of ownership over to him, with instructions to open it on the day after tomorrow if Carch didn't show up for work.

He wouldn't, of course. One way or another it would be all over tomorrow night. Either he'd be on his way to Galifrax, or he'd be dead. There was no compromise on that. No middle ground.

But Grodin was a loose cannon. The guy made him nervous.

Seri nodded. "He asked a lot of questions?"

"Yeah. Throwing him off with that famous author ruse was a great idea, but I'm not completely sure he bought it. I'm pretty sure he thinks I'm hiding something."

"Well, you are," she said with a wry smile. "He obviously has good instincts."

"What if he thinks I'm doing something illegal? Do you think he'll go to the authorities with his suspicions?" he asked nervously. "Or tell Williams?"

"Does it matter? You'll be light years away after tomorrow night." Something in her voice made him meet her

gaze. Was that regret that flared in her eyes before they skit
tered away?

"Angel," he said softly. But as much as he longed to, he
couldn't take her in his arms and tell her of his feelings, of how
desperate he was to have her come with him. He didn't dare

The traitor hadn't made himself known for a whole day
but Carch knew better than to think he'd given up. Tomorrow
after the exchange, he'd be there, waiting for his chance to kil
Carch and take the necklace. Carch wasn't planning to die
but if the worst happened, making declarations to her now
wouldn't be fair to her or her future.

Nevertheless, he wanted to spend as much time with her
as possible before that. Selfish? Oh, yeah. But he wasn't about
to let her out of his sight. Not for anything.

"Your aunt is fine," he murmured, brushing his fingertip
along her cheek. "Let's go home."

A rosy blush crept after his fingers and she bit her lip. She
knew exactly what he wanted, and he could feel the desire swir
through her body at his light touch. So why was she hesitating

"Please don't deny me now, when I need you most," he
whispered, his plea rife with that need. The need to be close
to her. The need to feel her warm, satiny body next to his. To
feel her amazing love for him steal through his consciousness
enveloping him, calming him, giving him courage from the
inside out. The courage to do what he must, even if it mean
losing her.

This time tomorrow, if he was still alive, he'd tell her. He'd
ask her to come with him.

But not today, not tonight. This one last day was theirs to
enjoy each other. To fit a lifetime of love into these few
precious hours, in case he wasn't around to share his with her

"I could never deny you, Carch," she whispered, and his
heart nearly broke.

Chapter 21

It was an afternoon Seri would never forget. Not as long as she lived. And the night was even more unforgettable.

It wasn't just the lovemaking that she and Carch shared—though goodness knows there was an abundance of hot, passionate lovemaking, slow, tender lovemaking, and everything in between. He changed his body to please her, worshipped hers as if she were a goddess, whispered erotic suggestions and sweet endearments in her ear, and did wonderful things to her that she'd never even imagined, let alone experienced.

But it was also all the other things they shared together when they were not making love that touched her heart. In bed they lounged and talked endlessly of his world and hers, of books they'd read and places they'd visited. They went down to his kitchen where they cooked their food naked, then ate in his opulent dining room feeling like naughty children. And afterwards they made love all over again.

It was all so perfect, so heart-wrenchingly perfect, that she wanted to cry. But as soon as she started to, as soon as her eyes felt the least bit misty, he was there kissing away the wistfulness and putting a smile back on her face.

She knew he could sense that tiny shadowed spot of agony growing in her mind over his leaving tomorrow. The emotion was too sharp, too persistent in her subconscious, too bald and ragged in its inevitability no matter how hard she tried to fight it, that he surely could not miss it.

And yet he did nothing, said nothing to soothe her heartache or calm her fears over their parting.

Other than to make sweet love to her again. And again.

So she resigned herself be swept away, reveling in the feel of his strong, hard body on hers, in hers, and drowned her ever-widening despair in the breathless sensuality of his taking.

He was hers now, tonight, and if that was all she'd be granted, she would not waste the precious minutes in useless misery.

"You've gotten quiet again," Carch murmured, weaving his fingers through hers as he lay on top of her. They had regained their breath after a long, slow buildup to their last climax. It was well after midnight and shadows danced on the wall from a lace curtain fluttering in a moonbeam.

She smiled up at him, loving how his weight felt pressing into her, loving how his muscular body made hers feel. Loving how *he* made her feel. "Just tired. We should probably get some sleep. Big day tomorrow."

A frown flitted across his forehead. "Yeah," he said with a sigh, and rolled off her. "I wish…" But he just shook his head and gathered her in his arms. "You're right. We should get some sleep."

She snuggled closer to him, warmed by his waning golden glow and cosseted by the mingled scents of their lovemaking lingering on tangled limbs and the tingle of energy humming around them. "Don't worry. It'll be okay. We'll get the necklace."

His arms tightened around her. "You mean *I* will. I want you to stay here while I make the exchange in the morning."

She lifted her head and looked at him. "Not a chance. You made me your ally, and you've got me. I'm in this till I see the red of your spaceship's taillights."

She thought she saw him wince. Then his distinctive features went authoritative in the semidarkness. "No. It's too dangerous."

"But you need me. What if—"

"This is not open for debate, Seri. You'll stay here and that's final."

"We'll see," she said, and kissed the hollow of his throat.

"Seri—"

"Shhh." She settled against him and closed her eyes, blanking her mind so he wouldn't sense her determination. "Sleep," she whispered.

Apparently the command worked—on her at least— because he let out a long breath and before it ended she had nodded off.

But the last thing she remembered thinking as she drifted into dreams was, damn, she'd forgotten to ask him about Aunt Tildy and Derrik.

Carch woke up early and slid silently out of bed. He hated leaving Seri, but he was determined to be dressed and gone before she awoke and demanded to come with him. He didn't want her anywhere near the exchange. He was too certain the traitor, whoever it was, would show up afterwards and try to take the necklace, using any means necessary.

He threw on his clothes and quickly padded downstairs to the kitchen with his toothbrush. Eyeing the coffeepot, he decided the noise of it would not be loud enough to wake her. Despite spending most of the previous day in bed, they'd gotten very little sleep. He needed to have his wits about him, and a little caffeine would go far.

He was just pouring his first cup when she walked into the kitchen wearing one of his shirts. It hit her about mid-thigh.

"Hope you made enough for me," she said sleepily, coming right to him for a hug. She was big on hugs, he'd noticed. He liked that about her. His own family wasn't overtly affectionate. Except for his mother. She liked hugs, too. Must be an Earth thing. It used to embarrass him to no end when his mom had demanded one from him, especially if there were others around to witness it. If he made it back to Galifrax alive, he vowed to hug his mother every single day, in front of the whole damn planet. And Seri, too. Because if he made it through today alive, there was no way in hell he was leaving her behind.

He returned her hug now, copping a feel and giving her a kiss for good measure. "What are you doing up so early? You should go back to bed."

"I could say the same thing. I know what you're trying to pull, spaceman, and it won't work. I told you I'm coming with you." She went up on her toes and kissed him back, as though that would settle it.

He poured her a cup of coffee, stalling until he could figure out a way to keep her away from the Thin Man Gallery and the exchange. But short of tying her to a bedpost, he couldn't think of a thing. She was maddeningly independent and strong-willed. Couldn't she understand he was only trying to keep her safe?

"Listen," she said, taking a sip. "I have something to ask you."

His heart stalled as he darted his gaze to her. *Uh-oh.*

Sure enough, her eyes were glued to the floor and she was biting her lip, a sure sign she was feeling vulnerable.

Ah, hell. Here it comes.

"Seri—"

"It's about King Derrik," she said, surprising him into silence.

"What about him?"

"Is he…? That is, does he…?" She looked up. "Do you think if Aunt Tildy went with you to Galifrax she would have a chance with him?" she blurted out, shocking him even more.

"Does she *want* to go?" he asked, irrationally annoyed that she was asking on her aunt's behalf, and not her own.

"She's still in love with him, Carch. After all these years. Of course she wants to go. But only if you think he'll want her. He *is* a widower, right?"

Carch wasn't really surprised. Every time the old dame talked about his grandfather there was a soft light in her eyes that was unmistakable. *Love.*

Kind of like the light that now shone in Seri's eyes. Was it for him? Or only for her aunt's happy ending? Why hadn't Seri told him *she* wanted to go with him? That *she* would finally accept his offer and be with him?

He wanted to grab her and shake her and demand she come with him. Demand she love him, as she had so sweetly asked him about his grandfather and her aunt. But he couldn't. Not yet…

However, once the Imperial Star was in his hands, all bets were off. He wasn't going to take no for an answer.

He tamped down his impatience and smiled. "There's a letter from the king in my jacket pocket. I meant to give it to Tildy yesterday. I have a feeling it's an invitation."

"Oh, Carch!" Seri threw her arms around his neck and kissed his cheek. "She'll be so happy."

The words of his own invitation burned on his tongue, but he refused to let them loose. He would *not* hurt her with promises he wasn't absolutely certain he could fulfill.

Soon...

He clamped his jaw and the moment drew out as she held him. The silence grew awkward. When she pulled away he knew he'd hurt her anyway. Her dashed hopes were written all over her disappointed face. She turned away quickly.

Damn it to Moradth!

Inwardly, he swore even more virulently, then turned on a toe and stalked over to a drawer, grabbing a pen and paper from it. Swiftly he scrawled out the place and time the transport ship would be landing to pick him up. He thrust it into her hand. "Bring her here tonight. But only if I get the Imperial Star. If I don't, all will be lost, and she will just provide further proof of my grandfather's supposed crimes. God knows what will happen to her if the traitor gets hold of her in that case."

Seri nodded solemnly, but still wouldn't meet his eyes. "I understand."

Devils of Taron, he felt like a royal bastard! It was pure torture to see her like this. Maybe he should just forget about his damned honor and tell her how he felt. Maybe he should—

Suddenly, there was a loud knock on the front door.

"Expecting someone?" she asked in a hushed voice as they both whirled toward the insistent sound, which quickly turned into pounding.

"No. You?"

"Are you kidding?"

"Charleston Police Department!" shouted a booming voice that was all too recognizable. "Carch Sunstryker, open this door!"

"Williams?" Seri whispered. "What the hell does he want?"

The pounding got even louder.

"God knows. But I'd better answer before they break it down."

Carch got to the door and flung it open just as Williams was issuing orders to his team to get the battering ram. "That won't be necessary," he said with a scowl. "What's this all about?"

The detective was wearing a poorly tailored blue suit and a smug smile that spelled trouble. With one hand he held up a wallet displaying his credentials, and with the other he passed Carch a folded piece of paper.

"Carch Sunstryker, you are under arrest on suspicion of trafficking in stolen goods. You'll have to come with us."

Chapter 22

"*What?* You can't do that!" Seri protested as Detective Williams slapped a pair of handcuffs onto Carch's wrists. "*Trafficking in stolen goods?* You have no evidence!"

"On the contrary. I have an eyewitness."

"Who?" she demanded when Carch said nothing other than muttering a string of oaths under his breath. "Obviously this so-called witness isn't who he says he is. He must be a—" A sharp look from Carch made her snap her mouth closed.

"A what, Miss Woodson?" Williams asked, cocking his head.

"An idiot. Or a liar. Carch sells books, not stolen goods. This is a witch hunt!"

"I guess we'll see about that. I have a team executing a search warrant on the Old World bookshop as we speak. Meanwhile, these officers will escort Mr. Sunstryker to Police Headquarters pending the results of the search. You may want to call his lawyer."

"I don't need a lawyer. I've done nothing wrong," Carch finally spoke up.

"And I suppose you'll deny working as a fence for the owners of the Thin Man Gallery, too."

"Of course he denies it!" Seri sputtered.

"Search all you like," Carch said, far too calmly for her taste. "You aren't going to find anything. Trust me, you won't make your case against them through me."

"If that's true, you have nothing to worry about," Williams said with a disbelieving sneer, pushing him out the door.

As two cops grabbed his arms, Carch glanced over his shoulder at her. "Seri, please extend my apologies to our friends we were meeting for breakfast. Remember it's my turn to treat. I believe I left my credit card at Tildy's place."

Breakfast? Anxiety zoomed through her. Oh, God! *He's telling me to get the necklace.* But what credit card did he mean? She'd never seen him use anything but cash. And the men they were dealing with certainly expected payment in cold, hard— "Carch, what—"

"And if I'm delayed, I trust you'll get Tildy to her appointment tonight," he added, his eyes burning with meaning.

Shock rooted her to the spot. Her lips parted. "You *can't* be delayed," she squeezed out from a tight throat. He *had* to get out of this in time to meet the transport. If he didn't…

"I wouldn't count on it," Williams cut in impatiently, beckoning the cops to get moving. "We have twenty-four hours to question him. And I'm confident we'll find the evidence we need to put him away for a lot longer than that."

She watched with a clash of conflicting emotions as Carch was led off—terror for his family if she and Tildy didn't somehow get the necklace back to Galifrax, but, to her shame, that noble sentiment battled with an overwhelming joy that he might be forced to stay here on Earth. With her.

"I'll see you later!" she called as he folded his tall frame into the backseat of the police car. He gave her one last smile, then the car door slammed and he was gone.

Oh. My. God.

What would she do now? *Think, girl!* But the only thing she could see in her mind was the complete trust in Carch's eyes as he'd smiled goodbye. He *trusted* her to do this. To fulfill his mission if he couldn't, and save his family from a horrible fate.

No pressure or anything.

Panic swept through her as she sprinted into his house to get dressed, trying to formulate a plan. First: get the necklace. Then: hide—

But wait! David and Alan expected money. A lot of it. Damn! She had to think logically, take things in order.

Where, oh, where were all her cool, scientific methods for coping with any and all situations when she needed them?

She threw on her clothes and ran to Carch's closet to find his jacket, to get the bundles of cash. Except the jacket wasn't there. Frantically she searched his dresser drawers. Nothing there, either. Where could he have—

Aunt Tildy's! That's what he'd meant about his credit card. He'd left his jacket and the money there.

She decided to take Carch's car to the Second Sun, so she could go straight to the police station after recovering the Imperial Star. No safer place to hide from an assassin than police headquarters. And then she'd also be around when they released Carch. Which they surely would. They *must*.

She parked, ran to the shop and tried to jerk the door open. It was locked. Her gaze swung to the obnoxious buzzers.

Aw, hell. *No time for this nonsense!* Closing her eyes briefly, she mashed the first one her fingers hit and leaned on it until her aunt stuck her head out the second-story window.

"Serenity June! What on earth is the matter?"

Seri winced when she realized which buzzer she'd been pushing. *Happiness and true love.*

Oh, God, not now. She couldn't think about love or she'd lose it completely.

"Let me in Aunt Tildy. They've arrested Carch!"

Carch gritted his teeth and glanced around the small, uncomfortably hot interrogation room in which he'd been left to stew. Could be worse. At least they hadn't booked him. He wasn't exactly sure how the legal system worked here, but he figured that meant this was just a fishing expedition by Williams. Which meant there was still a chance they'd let him go before tonight. Which in turn meant he wouldn't have to risk shapeshifting in order to get out of here—something he was technically forbidden to do because he'd noticed there were cameras everywhere, watching his every move. Picking locks for the camera was one thing. Shapeshifting was another entirely. Leaving that kind of irrefutable documentation of his patently alien abilities was almost as serious a crime as treason.

What a choice. Hang for breaking interplanetary law, or hang for treason.

He leaned his back against the hard cement wall instead of hitting it with his fist, which was what he really wanted to do.

And then there was Seri.

It made his blood boil thinking of her out there all on her own, pitted against the unknown traitor, risking her life and facing dangers that were rightly *his* to face.

Gods of Moradth. This was all his fault. If he'd done his job to begin with, secured the Imperial Star the first day he'd arrived on the planet and then lain low, none of this would be happening. The necklace would be safe. And so would Seri.

He squeezed his eyes shut, banking the terror that lay

just under the surface of his fury. If she was hurt... If anything happened to her... *If she ended up on that transport and he didn't...*

Damn it to hell! It didn't bear thinking about. None of those options were acceptable.

He looked around again, narrowing his gaze at the metal-encased all-seeing camera eye that stared down at him from the corner of the ceiling.

He had to get the hell out of here!

The question was, how?

"His jacket?" Aunt Tildy blinked at Seri. "I'm sure I don't remember seeing it anywhere in the shop or the apartment."

"But it has to be here," Seri insisted, her heartbeat kicking up. She *had* to find it—

"Maybe he put it with his duffel bag."

She halted in her frantic search behind the loveseat. "Duffel bag?"

Aunt Tildy nodded vigorously. "The one in the linen closet. He left it here when he first arrived. I assumed it was his spacesuit or something else he didn't need right now."

"Spacesuit?" Seri asked incredulously.

Aunt Tildy's face reddened and she shrugged. "Well, I didn't want to be nosy and ask."

"Show me," Seri demanded, and followed her to a built-in linen closet in the hall. On a shelf sat a largish navy blue canvas bag that looked for all the world like a small sailor's duffel. Whipping open the tie on top, she peered in.

And almost fell over.

"Holy—!"

Money. Stacks of it.

"Good lord, there must be a million dollars here!" Bundled by denomination. Mostly hundreds.

"Oh, my," Aunt Tildy said, ever the master of genteel understatement. "Well, I guess there'll be no problem paying David and Alan, then."

Seri wasn't going to think about where Carch had gotten so much Earth money. It looked real enough. She grabbed a couple of bundles and quickly counted out twenty thousand, the amount promised for the Imperial Star. Then she grabbed an extra for good measure.

She glanced at her watch. "It's late. I'd better get going."

"I'm coming with you," Aunt Tildy said, taking the money from her and tucking it into the front pockets of her long gypsy-style skirt. "They won't dare mess with me."

Despite everything, Seri grinned and gave her aunt a hug. "Thanks. I know I shouldn't involve you, but I could use the moral support."

"As if I'd let you go alone," Aunt Tildy declared with a harrumph. "Come on. They'll be waiting."

Seri could only hope.

She and her aunt hurried out of the Second Sun and crossed the courtyard. She forced herself to ignore the grim policeman standing guard at the back entrance to the Old World bookshop. She prayed the cops' presence hadn't scared David and Alan into staying away from the Thin Man. She didn't know what she'd do if they didn't show up.

As they passed the Palmistry Shoppe, Madam Clarissa appeared at the door, hands on her hips.

"Where are you ladies off to in such a hurry?" she called out shrilly, attracting the policeman's attention as well as their own. Clarissa eyed the Thin Man's display windows, then swung her prying gaze back to them. "Doings at the gallery this morning I don't know about?"

"Good morning, Clarissa," Aunt Tildy greeted her cheerfully, giving the cop a wave, too. Seri almost choked when her aunt went on to lie blithely, "No, no. David thinks he may have spotted my necklace at a pawn shop. Isn't that wonderful? We're just going over to get the information."

The big black tom cat trotted out from Clarissa's shop and sat at her feet, its long tail flicking back and forth, watchful yellow eyes tracking their movements as closely as its mistress's. It was joined by two other cats, who rubbed up against Clarissa's legs, yowling.

Seri suppressed a shudder as she turned away. And to think she'd always loved cats before.

The Thin Man was open when they tried the door. A good sign. They entered the shop and immediately Alan ushered them into the office in back. His hands fluttered nervously. Despite the cool air conditioning, his forehead held a sheen of perspiration.

"I declare, all these cops everywhere! I'm a nervous wreck," he confessed in a strained, high-pitched voice. "What has your boyfriend done? Murdered someone?"

"Not yet," she answered evenly, causing his eyes to widen to saucers. "But I wouldn't tempt him. Where's the necklace?"

David was sitting at his desk. He rose now. "What about the money?"

"We have it," she assured him. Aunt Tildy patted her skirt pocket.

He gave a curt nod. "Good. The sooner I get rid of this distasteful thing the better. I'm sorry we ever found it."

Seri's mouth dropped open.

"You found it?" Aunt Tildy asked, obviously as surprised as Seri was. Good grief. In their cover conversation yesterday she had actually stumbled on the truth!

"In the courtyard," Alan said. "Under that big gardenia you're always watering out there."

Aunt Tildy gave Seri a baleful, apologetic look. She shook her head. "Not to worry."

"But why didn't you return it?" Aunt Tildy asked David, her voice suffused with hurt.

"I wish to God we had," he said, grimacing. "It's been bad juju from the second we found it."

"Bad juju?"

"Like the thing is genuinely cursed."

Interesting. Carch had said its powers were strong, so Seri shouldn't be surprised it had shown its displeasure at their unethical moves. But she *was* surprised. She supposed she hadn't really believed Carch when he'd told her that an inanimate object could possess supernatural powers. It was hard enough just believing in *his* powers, despite seeing them with her own eyes—and feeling them with her own body—

But no. She wasn't going there.

Aunt Tildy handed the money to Alan, who thumbed through it counting madly as David dropped the necklace onto Seri's palm.

"There. Take it. And good riddance. Get it the hell out of here."

He'd get no argument from her. She and Aunt Tildy left the office. They'd made it as far as the middle of the gallery when a rush of…something that felt like pure white energy surged through her hand and up through her entire body.

She cried out, thrusting the necklace at Aunt Tildy. But it was too late. A vision swirled through her mind, clear as day and sharp as a nightmare.

She saw Carch. They were in a green meadow that smelled of newly mown grass. He was striding away from her. Toward a huge, golden spacecraft. She was crying, desperate to call him back. Or to go with him. But he kept walking up, up, up a steep floating ramp that disappeared into the ship. Without her.

She screamed, "*Carch!*"

He didn't look back. The spacecraft door shut behind him. Then with a mighty wind that whipped the grass and the trees around the meadow into a froth, the golden ship silently rose into the sky and, in the blink of an eye, it vanished.

And just like that, the man she loved was gone.

Gone forever.

Chapter 23

"You have two minutes."

Carch wanted to argue with the guard who had given the order, but he held his tongue. He was lucky to get to see Seri at all. The only reason he'd been granted this tiny reprieve was that the watch captain's wife was a long-time client of Tildy's and had used her influence on her husband. Carch wasn't about to waste his precious two minutes arguing for more.

He strode into the small room where Seri was waiting, and she launched herself into his arms.

"Oh, Carch. I can't believe they're doing this. How are you?"

He kissed her and rocked her in a tight embrace, then held her away so he could look into her eyes. "I'm okay. You?"

She nodded, gnawing her lower lip. "Okay."

"Tildy?"

"Good. She got her necklace back."

He gripped her arms, not quite letting himself feel relief. "She put it in a safe place?"

"Around her neck. Then we came straight here. To the police station." Seri's eyes sought approval.

He swallowed. "Okay. Yeah. Probably as safe as it gets."

She gnawed harder, looking as if she was barely keeping it together. "We'll be waiting here when you're released."

"All right." Given the uncertainties of the situation it was the last thing he wanted, but he forced himself to say, "But whatever you do, don't miss that appointment tonight."

He sensed a wave of tangled emotions shudder through her. Her beautiful eyes grew shiny, rimmed with anxiety. "We won't," she whispered. "But—"

Her chaotic feelings were impossible for him to decipher in his own muddied state of mind, but he felt instinctively he was at the center of them all. "Seri, please don't worry about me. You know what's most important here. You know what's at stake. I'm counting on you."

She reluctantly nodded, and a single tear trailed down her cheek. "I know."

"Nothing else matters right now."

"I understand."

Did she? He didn't think so. "One way or another, I'll be there," he assured her, pulling her into his arms again.

"Yes, I know you will."

A tremor passed through her body and he was swamped by a deluge of misery that emanated from deep inside her. He sucked down a breath, alarmed by the fierceness of the emotion. He opened his mouth to ask her what was going on, but just then the guard took her arm and yanked her from him.

"Time's up. Let's go, miss."

"Seri!" he called after her. But the door banged shut and it was too late.

"Damn!"

What the hell was wrong?

Why had she reacted like that? Was she hiding something? *Did she know something he didn't?*

He'd been biding his time here in the jail, tolerating the endless, meaningless questions being asked over and over again and going nowhere. Waiting for his chance to escape. But now he was galvanized.

Something was definitely wrong. He could feel it in his bones.

And he wasn't about to leave Seri to face whatever it was alone.

Crime or no, and despite the danger and the risk, he had no choice. He had to shift, and get the hell out of there.

And he had to do it soon.

The afternoon dragged on and on. Every fifteen minutes or so, Seri faithfully trooped over to the duty sergeant and inquired as to when Carch would be released. The good sergeant was pretty annoyed with her by now, so she made sure she was always excruciatingly polite. She had little doubt he'd arrest her just so he could banish her from his cramped waiting room.

She watched with trepidation as the clock marched forward, closer and closer to the appointed time to meet the transport ship, while Aunt Tildy sat with her eyes closed, uncharacteristically quiet.

At length her aunt cracked open her eyelids, sighed and said, "We should eat."

They'd skipped lunch, and come to think of it neither of them had eaten breakfast, either. Still…

"I don't think I could eat a bite. And what if they let him go while we're gone?"

"We'll need our strength for tonight," Aunt Tildy said quietly but firmly.

Seri's pulse kicked up. "Have you seen…? Has the necklace…?" She stopped herself before asking if it had sent her aunt a vision, too. When that had happened to her this morning, at Aunt Tildy's questions she'd pretended it was an anxiety attack. No way could she admit to having visions. Hello? That went against every scientific principle she'd ever believed.

But then…so did loving a man from outer space.

"Has the necklace what?" her aunt asked, brow raised.

Seri straightened her spine and took a deep breath. This was Aunt Tildy. Of all people, she wouldn't think she was crazy. "Has it told you anything…with its powers? About the future?"

Her aunt's other brow flew up. "What?"

Oh, damn! She'd forgotten Aunt Tildy knew nothing about its special powers.

Her aunt stared at her for the longest time. Then she sighed. "Well, that explains it. I'm not the least bit psychic, am I? It's always been the Imperial Star guiding my tarot readings."

Seri took her hand and held it between hers. "I don't know, Aunt Tildy. Carch didn't really explain any of that."

"It's okay," her aunt said. "I guess I've really always known. I never had those kinds of leanings before Derrik gave me the necklace. I wanted to believe that loving him had somehow changed me inside. Given me the talent. He was an empath, you know."

Seri nodded. Like his grandson. "It did change you, Aunt Tildy." As loving Carch had changed her. No, not by becoming psychic, but in other, more profound ways.

Her aunt gripped her hand, laying her other one on top of it. "I've decided I'm going to him," she said. "To Derrik. On Galifrax."

Seri smiled. "I know." There hadn't really ever been any doubt about that.

"You must come, too," her aunt urged.

She wanted to. So much. But she was deathly afraid of making a terrible mistake—and a huge fool of herself. She shook her head. "I don't know…"

"Carch loves you. Anyone can see that."

"I don't think so." After those awkward moments this morning, she was sure he didn't. She dropped her gaze to the floor so her aunt wouldn't see the pain in her eyes. "He still hasn't said anything."

"Oh, sweetheart. I'm sure he just hasn't dared. Not until he was sure he had a future to invite you to share. But now we have the Imperial Star safe and sound, he'll beg you to come with him. I just know it."

"If he ever gets out of this jail," she murmured under her breath, nevertheless feeling a slight trickle of hope. Maybe her aunt was right. Maybe he was just waiting for the right moment. If so, he'd better hurry the hell up.

"He will," Aunt Tildy said, then stood up with a smile. "Let's go pack our bags, darling. It's time."

The old black tom was sitting in his spot on the wooden courtyard bench when Seri and her aunt cautiously poked their heads out from the Second Sun after collecting the things Aunt Tildy wanted to take with her to Galifrax. Seri had decided not to pack. The odds were stacked too high against her.

Suddenly, two other cats streaked across the bricks past her ankles. She jumped, grabbing her thundering heart. She really had to calm down.

Her aunt had managed to talk the duty sergeant into sending them home in a patrol car—so they could leave Carch's car for him—but as soon as they'd gotten out the officer had driven away, leaving no one to protect them should they run afoul of the traitor.

Her nerves were shot.

She needed Carch. *Where was he?*

"Skipping town, ladies?"

She whirled, recognizing John Grodin's voice behind her. "What are you doing here?" she demanded, putting herself between him and Aunt Tildy—and the necklace.

Carch seemed to trust the guy, but at the moment she suspected everyone of being the traitor. And it was peculiar how he always seemed to turn up, like a bad penny.

Speaking of which… She glanced around. But the cats had vanished.

"Hello, John," her aunt greeted the reporter easily while pulling the door to the Second Sun closed for the final time. Without looking back, Aunt Tildy turned and wrestled her rolling suitcase onto the cobblestone path in front of the shop.

Grodin courteously took the handle from her and set it right. Seri narrowed her eyes, even more suspicious.

"Just checking in to see if there have been any further developments." Grodin gave them a guileless smile. "In the robbery case."

"Well, as a matter of fact—" her aunt started.

"Aunt Tildy!" Seri exclaimed, cutting off what she'd been about to say. "Do you really think—"

Her aunt waved her hand. "Oh, pish, my dear. Mr. Grodin is not a bad guy. Are you, Mr. Grodin?"

"I still don't—"

But before she could finish her protest, Aunt Tildy turned to him. "Would you do us a huge favor, Mr. Grodin, and serve as our bodyguard for an hour or so? You see, I got my necklace back, but we have reason to believe someone will try to take it from me again."

"Really?" he said, his reporter's ears perking up. "Why would you think that?"

"Just a feeling," Seri interrupted. No way should they share even a hint of the truth. Not that any sane person would actually believe them. But then, reporters didn't have to believe. They merely reported.

Imagine what would happen if Grodin followed them and managed to get photos of the Fracian transport ship.

Yikes.

"Look, never mind. We've already called a taxi," Seri said, deliberately easing Aunt Tildy along the path toward the street. Damn. It had been a real mistake not bringing Carch's car.

"Nonsense," Grodin returned, grabbing the tapestry carpetbag Seri was carrying for her aunt. "I'll be happy to drive you wherever you need to go. Where to? The airport?"

Oh, what the hell. They'd never shake him anyway. And if he was going to kill them, he'd probably have done it by now.

"Not exactly," Seri answered warily.

The spaceship was scheduled to land in an obscure, deserted area after dark. Already the sun had gone down and the red-orange dusk was turning to indigo. They needed to hurry. "We're, um, meeting someone up by Joe Riley Stadium."

Which was where Charleston's minor league baseball team, the Riverdogs, played. The rendezvous was out in a no-man's-land of marshland past the parking lots and, conveniently for Carch's present predicament, the police station. She prayed he had somehow already escaped and was waiting for them there.

"Okay. Of course I know where the Joe is," Grodin said, looking more and more intrigued and less and less like a villain.

She wondered briefly if shapeshifters could only shift their outward physical appearance, or if they had the ability to mask their inner self, too. Their true personality and agenda. If so, she and Aunt Tildy were in big trouble here.

Against Seri's instincts, they accepted Grodin's offer.

He led them to a beat-up Camry parked on a nearby side street, setting Aunt Tildy's bags in the backseat next to her while Seri slid into the front passenger seat—after carefully checking to make sure the door handle worked. It did.

Paranoid? Her?

Her foot knocked against a camera—a good-quality digital Nikon as it turned out—sitting on the floor. Another indication he was legit. Or maybe put there precisely to make her think that. Damn. She was totally psyching herself out. But there was one thing she could do.

As he expertly threaded the Camry through the ever-darkening maze of narrow one-way streets that made the peninsula so hard for outsiders to navigate, she managed to pull the camera up by the strap and relieve it of its memory card, which she dropped under the seat. If nothing else, at least that should take care of any unwanted evidence of UFOs on tomorrow's front page of the *Post and Courier*.

When they arrived at the dead end that marked the edge of the marshy meadow next to the river, Grodin gave Seri a doubtful look. "Are you sure this is where you're meeting your friends?"

She nodded. "I know it's a bit out of the way."

"More like downright dangerous," he muttered. "It's almost dark. This place is a mugging waiting to happen, or worse. You do realize I can't let you and Miss Tildy hang around here by yourselves?"

Who said chivalry was dead? Unfortunately, she didn't quite know what to do about his untimely gallantry, short of conking the man over the head with his camera.

If it really was chivalry…

Nobody else had followed them here. Yet it was unlikely the traitor had given up. Was Grodin the bad guy, after all?

Okay, duh. Having probably come here on the same transport as Carch, the traitor must already know about the rendezvous and was even now lying in wait for them somewhere in the park....

Not a cheery thought.

"You shouldn't stick around," she told Grodin. "These people are pretty adamant about their privacy. If they find out you're a reporter, well, who knows what they'll do." Which was true enough.

"Which people?" he asked, in true reporter style.

Aunt Tildy leaned in conspiratorially. "They're not actually people. They're aliens. From the planet Galifrax. We're meeting their spaceship."

Grodin blinked. His gaze cut to Seri.

She smiled. He wasn't the only one who could do guileless.

"I see," he said.

She hoped not. But without evidence, who would believe him? No one had believed Aunt Tildy for forty-two years. Including Seri.

If his expression of incredulity was anything to go by, Grodin really was innocent.

She grabbed the suitcases from him with one hand. "Don't worry. We'll be fine." She took her aunt's arm with the other and headed into the park, leaving Grodin to stay or go as he pleased. In the distance, a cat yowled.

An air current kicked up and stirred the leaves of the trees. She shivered, recalling her earlier vision. And realized her whole body was trembling.

She longed to see Carch's long-legged stride coming toward them. But what if the vision came true?

No. She couldn't think about that right now. Couldn't think about how much she loved him and wanted to go with him. How much she needed him to say he loved her, too.

No. Getting Aunt Tildy safely on board with the necklace was the first priority. Everything else was secondary.

Including her desperate heart.

They trudged onward, through a fringe of moss-draped oaks and elegant willows, emerging onto the rim of a meadow filled with tall, fragrant grasses. Just like the one in her vision.

All at once a swirling wind whipped the trees and grass into a frenzy of motion. She dropped the suitcases and hugged Aunt Tildy close.

Omigod. This was it!

The air shimmered in a muted golden light and slowly a giant, silent presence filled the meadow before them. It wasn' completely visible, not quite, more like a mirage hovering above the ground. And then it delicately settled down, crushing the vegetation and filling the air with the distinctive scent of newly mown grass. Just like her vision.

She watched in hypnotic wonder as the spaceship material ized before her eyes, golden and elegant, filled with flashing lights and dark, mysterious voids. And then a long, narrow ramp floated out from a black archway that yawned open in the hull.

Behind her, a deep, familiar voice said contently, "Righ on time."

Chapter 24

"Carch!" Seri spun around and wrapped her arms around his neck and pressed her nose into the shoulder of his jacket. The familiar scent of him embraced her, even if he didn't. "Oh, Carch, I was so afraid you wouldn't make it!"

She reached up to kiss him, but he just gave her a quick squeeze and let her go, saying, "You have the Imperial Star? Where is it?"

"Right here," Aunt Tildy said, her hand fluttering at the base of her throat. She tore her gaze from the huge spacecraft before them. "Thank goodness you've come."

It was the first time Seri had ever seen her aunt look frightened. It took her aback.

Carch glanced backward as though expecting trouble. "Good. Let me have it, then."

"No need," Aunt Tildy said tremulously. "I'm coming with you."

"What?" He looked oddly surprised.

Suddenly cats were everywhere. A half dozen or more ran into the meadow, scampering around everyone's legs, jumping onto the ramp. One launched itself at Carch, tearing at his jacket ferociously with its sharp teeth. An envelope fell out of the jacket pocket.

He swore, batting the cat away with his forearm. "Damn beast! All right," he yelled, grabbing Aunt Tildy's arm. "Let's go then!"

She balked. "But what about Seri?"

He hesitated a split second, then turned back to Seri. "Serenity June. What can I say? You're an amazing woman. I'll always be grateful for everything you did for me. Thank you so much." Once again he took her aunt's arm and started hurrying away from Seri.

Hello?

Her jaw dropped.

Thank you?

Her body froze where she stood.

Thank you?

Oh, God. He was kissing her off! He wasn't going to beg her to come with him. He wasn't even going to ask. *He didn't care that he was leaving her behind.*

The realization that the man she loved didn't love her back, didn't even want her, hit Seri like a nuclear explosion to her heart. Her insides ripped apart in a million pieces, razored to shreds.

She swallowed heavily.

She would not cry. She *would not.*

"You're welcome," she managed to tell his quickly retreating back.

Aunt Tildy's expression registered shock. "But Carch…" She broke loose and ran back to Seri, embraced her in a crushing hug. "We can't leave—"

"No time for this! Let's go. The ship must take off immediately." He strode back and yanked Aunt Tildy away, swiped up her suitcases and hustled her up the floating ramp, kicking off a big yellow tabby that got in his way.

The cat tumbled to the ground, spun, then charged back up after them. Seri tried to find the voice to warn Carch.

But she couldn't speak a word. She was too stunned by his coldness. Too gutted by his betrayal.

With a last worried glance backward, Aunt Tildy was pushed through the doorway and disappeared into the spacecraft, followed closely by Carch. The black opening slammed shut behind them with a metallic, echoing clang.

Then the golden ship rose silently into the sky and in the blink of an eye, it vanished.

Gone.

She couldn't believe it.

He'd left her.

They'd both left her.

The two people she loved most in the world. *Gone forever.*

Just like in her vision.

Except… What was that? She walked over to the envelope that had fallen out of Carch's pocket and picked it up. On the outside in an authoritative hand was written *For Tildy Woodson.*

Envelope in hand, she tilted her face up to the sky. The stars had blurred to streaks. Already she missed her aunt so very much. With trembling fingers, Seri slit open the envelope and took out the single sheet of thick cream vellum crowned with a royal seal among a spangling of glittering golden stars.

My Dearest Love,

It is with the greatest joy and anticipation that I send my only grandson back to Earth to fulfill the destiny you and I began so many years ago. I can scarcely believe the time has finally arrived, and I shall see you soon!

Meeting you, my dearest Tildy, taught me so much. About myself, about loyalty, about the enduring nature of love.

I trust the vision of the future given to me by the Imperial Star has proven true, and that Prince Carch will hasten home with the future queen of Galifrax by his side, a woman of strength, beauty and compassion. A woman who will help us rule with wisdom.

Come to me, Tildy my love. I await you.

Derrik

Seri's throat tightened around a sob. *So beautiful.* So everything she had hoped Carch would say to her. Would feel about her.

But hadn't.

She was so happy for Aunt Tildy. She deserved every minute of the joyous future she would surely find with the man who wrote this wonderful letter.

She smoothed it in her hand and wrapped her arms around her middle, fighting the horrible, involuntary pain that clawed through her at the thought of the future.

A future without Carch.

Her eyes filled.

But she would not cry. *She would not cry.*

It was her own fault. That's what she got for letting her guard down. For letting herself feel. For letting herself love.

Love brought pain. Nothing but pain.

"Are you okay?" Grodin came running up behind her, white as a ghost in the moonlight. "Sweet jeezus, did you see that thing? What in sweet blazes was it?"

She took a deep, steadying breath and turned to see the

reporter halt next to her, eyeing his camera and shaking it in annoyance.

"What thing?" she asked, drawing calmness from a well-spring of strength she didn't know she had.

Carch Sunstryker might have broken her heart, crushed her feelings, betrayed her trust, but she, Serenity June Woodson, was better than that. She would not betray him, or his damn alien secrets.

"Why, that huge…UFO!" Grodin pointed up in the air, waving his arms and camera wildly.

"Oh, you mean the helicopter that just picked up my aunt," she said, determinedly ignoring the knife blade of hurt that sliced through her already devastated heart. "Probably just looked big with the lights reflecting off the tree leaves."

Grodin gaped at her as though she were nuts. "You're telling me that was—" His mouth suddenly snapped shut and his eyes went wide as dinner plates. "Aw, hell, you're one of them!" He slowly backed away from her, then whirled and ran, hard, for his car.

She shuddered out a breath.

She would not cry. *She would not cry.*

A couple of the cats trotted out of the darkness and rubbed up against her legs. She looked down at them and sighed. "So I guess you guys weren't aliens, after all," she murmured past her tight throat.

They looked up at her and blinked.

And that's when she burst into tears.

After docking, Carch trotted straight to his quarters on the big sci-cruiser, darting from shadow to shadow, running along the narrow corridors and past a few of his surprised ship-mates. When he got to his cabin door, he came to a sliding halt and looked around for help. Luckily, one of his best friends, Luthrek, was coming out of his cabin two doors down. He yelled to him, frustrated when it came out as a garbled yodel.

Luthrek took one searching look down at him, and said, "Carch? But—"

Carch yowled, twitching his feline tail frantically. Every minute wasted was a minute more the traitor had to wreak havoc in Carch's own image, spreading his treasonous poison against King Derrik. And every minute sent the ship hurtling farther and farther away from the Earth. And Seri.

What must she be thinking?

He couldn't—he mustn't—think about that now. He must secure his family's future first. But after that, no matter what it took, he was damn well going back to secure his own future.

Impatiently he waited for Luthrek to sprint over and let him into the cabin. Carch went directly to the bed and jumped up on it. And landed on his own jacket. The bastard had stolen it! So that was how he'd fooled Seri. She would have recognized his smell and never questioned whether it was him.

"Gods of Moradth, Carch," Luthrek muttered. "If you're the prince, who the hell is on the bridge talking with the captain?"

Carch let out a grateful meow before gathering all his concentration, squeezing his eyes shut and willing the process to begin. Shifting appearances was always painful for him. Going from human to cat had been excruciating, but he'd had no choice. It was the only way he could think of to escape from the jail and make it to the ship on time. He'd had to knock out the guard who'd been taking him from the interrogation room, duck out of sight of the surveillance cameras and shift quickly. Shifting back within such a short time would be even worse. And he was already exhausted, nearly at the end of his strength.

For the next fifteen minutes he literally walked through the fires of nebular hell. When he came out the other side, Luthrek was there with a warm, wet towel and a fortifying drink.

"Steady there, mate."

His abused body trembling, Carch threw back the brew and stumbled to his feet. "Got to stop him. The traitor has the Imperial Star. Is the old woman unharmed?"

"She's fine, except for a nasty scratch on her neck," his friend said as he tossed an officer's uniform at him from the closet. "She's a feisty old bird. Kept saying you weren't you. Couldn't be. Something about a niece."

Despite the pain wracking his body, Carch grinned as he pulled on his uniform. "Tildy's got good instincts." And they had nothing to do with the powers of the necklace. "She'll make us a damn fine queen."

He swept out of his cabin, Luthrek at his side, gathering a small army of crew and scientists as he strode swiftly to the bridge.

When they got there, it was no contest. The traitor didn't even try to deny he wasn't Carch. With a shimmer of gold, the man shifted back to his real body, one of King Derrik's trusted advisors.

"Prince Carch is the traitor!" he cried, his voice eerily similar to that of Detective Williams. "He stole a sacred Galifracian treasure, the Imperial Star, and took it off the planet. Arrest him!"

The crowd murmured in shock and uncertainty. The captain turned to him. "Is this true, my lord?"

Williams. He should have guessed as much when the man had shielded his thoughts so easily. Carch narrowed his eyes at the traitor who, for the sake of power and greed, would have seen Carch's grandfather and his whole family executed. "No," he said with jaw clenched. "He is the one who has the necklace. Search him and you'll find it."

The traitor sputtered and protested his innocence when the guards, indeed, found both the Imperial Star and its duplicate tucked in an inside pocket of his uniform.

"Arrest him," Carch ordered, and watched in grim distaste as the man was led away in chains. Slowly, he let out the breath it seemed as though he'd been holding since running up that floating ramp, leaving behind the woman he loved. He faced the captain. "You must turn the ship around immediately. We're going back."

"To Earth? That's not possible," the captain protested.

Carch ground his jaw, reining in the urge to throttle the man. He didn't understand. This was not open to debate. "Turn the ship around," he said between his clenched teeth, "or I'll do it myself."

The captain drew himself to his full, commanding height. "May I ask why, my lord?"

They didn't have time for this! Carch thought of Seri, her beautiful face, her irritating independence, her endearing laugh, her unwavering loyalty, the devastation in her eyes when his evil doppelganger cast her aside without a second thought. He couldn't bear the thought that she was in pain because of him.

"There's someone we have to pick up," he snapped.

"Who?" the captain demanded.

Carch's heart swelled with certainty. Suddenly he couldn't keep the joyful smile from his face. He wanted her to be with him forever. To bear his children, to grow old with him in his family's castle on the edge of the white cliffs overlooking the blue-green Eldor Sea. To be his till the stars faded.

When he answered the captain, it was in a booming voice loud enough for the whole damn universe to hear.

"We're going back to fetch my wife!"

Seri trudged slowly through the midnight courtyard toward the depressingly empty and uninviting Second Sun Crystal and Tarot Salon. Despite the sultry air, she shivered. All the windows were dark around the circle of brick buildings. Not even the Thin Man Gallery was lit up as it usually was. She wondered if the police had finally arrested David and Alan. Or maybe they'd hightailed it out of town.

Like a certain someone else.

Closing her eyes, she fought the unwelcome emotions that threatened to overtake her again. A soft, silky presence pressed itself against her ankles. She picked up the old black tom and scratched his neck with a watery laugh. "Boy, did I get it wrong," she murmured, burying her face in his fluffy fur as she gave him a hug. "Everything. Completely, utterly wrong."

The tom wriggled, and she set him down. He shook her off, trotting away, head high, without a backward glance.

Just as Carch had done.

She still couldn't believe how cold and callous he'd been, walking away from her. Like a different person altogether.

Halting for a brief second, she gazed after the cat…then shook her head. No. That was her breaking heart talking. Not reason or rationality.

It *was* Carch on that ramp. She'd even recognized the smell of his jacket. It had to have been him. And he'd left her behind without even breaking stride.

Face reality, girl. He didn't want you. Not like she'd wanted him. He'd only been interested in a few days of uncomplicated sex.

She swiped angrily at the single tear that escaped. She couldn't believe she'd allowed herself to be fooled so badly. All the signs had been there, but she'd been blinded by her unfamiliar feelings. He'd never said he loved her. Never said he wanted her to marry him. Never said he wanted to spend his life with her.

Never.

It had all been her own sadly deluded heart's fault.

But no more.

From now on, it was back to science and logic for her. No more forays into the murky, painful depths of emotional involvement. No, sir.

She reached the Second Sun, and stalled when she saw the buzzers lined up next to the front door.

Press me if you're feeling blue.

...if your goal is fame and fortune.

...if you seek to find happiness and true love.

...if revenge or protection is your greatest wish.

Press me if you long to be reunited with the one you loved and lost.

Which one should she press tonight?

She lifted her hand, aiming for the top buzzer. At the last moment it wavered, seeking the bottom one of its own volition.

Her vision blurred.

Oh, God. She swallowed a sob.

How could he have left her all alone?

Determinedly, she moved her finger back up to the top one and started to push.

"You could choose that one," a deep, lovingly familiar and achingly tender voice said behind her.

Suddenly, she couldn't breathe.

Impossible!

"But I was hoping," his voice continued, "you might try the third buzzer this time."

Happiness and true love?

Could it be? Brilliant, delirious hope surged through her. Had he changed his mind and come back for her, after all?

Hot trails of moisture slid silently down her cheeks, tasting of salt and bewildered joy. "Not the last button?" she managed to ask past the moon-sized lump in her throat. "About the one I loved and lost?"

"Hell, no." She felt his warm, hard body move up behind hers. His breath tickled her neck and ear. "You never lost me, my angel. And you better still love me. I need you with me."

"But…but you said…"

His arms came around her, pulling her close to his chest. "Not me. I should be insulted," he scolded softly. "Since when have I ever called you Serenity June?"

Her heart soared, bursting from her chest in happiness. She turned in his arms, gazing up at his wonderful, beloved face. His *real* face—strong and golden and looking down at her with so much love she could never doubt the depth of his feelings for her, not ever again.

"He was the traitor." She put her hands to his broad chest. "Oh, Carch, I should have listened to my instincts. They were telling me it wasn't you. But I didn't trust them. I just couldn't believe—"

"Hush," he said, lowering his mouth to hers. "Listen to them now. What are they telling you?"

She wrapped her arms around his neck, held him close, so very close, and whispered, "To shut up and kiss you. And never let you go."

"Mmm," he murmured, his lips forming a smile against hers as she did just that. "Very good instincts, my love."

"I love you, Carch. So much."

He kissed her long and tenderly. And when he lifted his head he whispered, "I love you, too, Seri. More than anything else in the universe."

And that's when she knew she believed in him. In destiny. And in her one true love. A love that would last forever.

A love that was written in the stars.

* * * * *

Look for Nina Bruhns's next sexy and suspenseful
Silhouette Romantic Suspense novel,
KILLER TEMPTATION,
book 1 of the new SEDUCTION SUMMER
continuity series, available in June 2008!

Enjoy a sneak preview of
MATCHMAKING WITH A MISSION
by B.J. Daniels,
part of the WHITEHORSE, MONTANA *miniseries.*
Available from Harlequin Intrigue
in April 2008.

Nate Dempsey has returned to Whitehorse to uncover the truth about his past...

Nate sensed someone watching the house and looked out in surprise to see a woman astride a paint horse just on the other side of the fence. He quickly stepped back from the filthy second-floor window, although he doubted she could have seen him. Only a little of the June sun pierced the dirty glass to glow on the dust-coated floor at his feet as he waited a few heartbeats before he looked out again.

The place was so isolated he hadn't expected to see another soul. Like the front yard, the dirt road was waist-high with weeds. When he'd broken the lock on the back door, he'd had to kick aside a pile of rotten leaves that had blown in from last fall.

As he sneaked a look, he saw that she was still there,

staring at the house in a way that unnerved him. He shielded his eyes from the glare of the sun off the dirty window and studied her, taking in her head of long blond hair that feathered out in the breeze from under her Western straw hat.

She wore a tan canvas jacket, jeans and boots. But it was the way she sat astride the brown-and-white horse that nudged the memory.

He felt a chill as he realized he'd seen her before. In that very spot. She'd been just a kid then. A kid on a pretty paint horse. Not this one—the markings were different. Anyway, it couldn't have been the same horse, considering the last time he had seen her was more than twenty years ago. That horse would be dead by now.

His mind argued it probably wasn't even the same girl. But he knew better. It was the way she sat on the horse, so at home in a saddle and secure in her world on the other side of that fence.

To the boy he'd been, she and her horse had represented freedom, a freedom he'd known he would never have—even after he escaped this house.

Nate saw her shift in the saddle, and for a moment he feared she planned to dismount and come toward the house. With Ellis Harper in his grave, there would be little to keep her away.

To his relief, she reined her horse around and rode back the way she'd come.

As he watched her ride away, he thought about the way she'd stared at the house—today and years ago. While the smartest thing she could do was to stay clear of this house, he had a feeling she'd be back.

Finding out her name should prove easy, since he figured she must live close by. As for her interest in Harper House… He would just have to make sure it didn't become a problem.

* * * * *

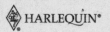

Love Inspired.
HISTORICAL

INSPIRATIONAL HISTORICAL ROMANCE

Maddie Norton's life was devoted to her simple yet enduring faith, to good works and to the elderly lady whose companion she was. She believed herself content. But then her mistress's handsome nephew returned home. As she came to know this man better, she began to wonder if two solitary souls might yet find new life—and love—as one.

Look for

Hearts in the Highlands

by

RUTH AXTELL MORREN

Steeple
Hill®

Available April wherever books are sold.

www.SteepleHill.com

LIH82786

HARLEQUIN

"The more I see, the more I feel the need."

—**Aviva Presser,** real-life heroine

*Aviva Presser is a Harlequin More Than Words
award winner and the founder of **Bears Without Borders**.*

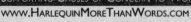

REQUEST YOUR FREE BOOKS!

2 FREE NOVELS PLUS 2 FREE GIFTS!

Silhouette® Romantic

SUSPENSE

Sparked by Danger, Fueled by Passion!

nocturne™

The Bloodrunners
trilogy continues with book #2.

The hunt meant more to Jeremy Burns than dominance—
it meant facing the woman he left behind. Once
Jillian Murphy had belonged to Jeremy, but now she was
the Spirit Walker to the Silvercrest wolves. It would take
more than the rights of nature for Jeremy to renew his
claim on her—and she would not go easily once he had.

LAST WOLF HUNTING

by RHYANNON BYRD

Available in April wherever books are sold.

Be sure to watch out for the last book,
Last Wolf Watching, available in May.

SN61785

Silhouette®
Romantic
SUSPENSE

COMING NEXT MONTH

#1507 DANGER SIGNALS—Kathleen Creighton
The Taken

Detective Wade Callahan is determined to discover the killer in a string of unsolved murders—without the help of his new partner. Tierney Doyle is used to being criticized for her supposed psychic abilities, but even the tough-as-nails—and drop-dead-gorgeous—detective can't deny what she has uncovered. And Tierney is slowly discovering that working so closely to Wade could be lethal.

#1508 A HERO TO COUNT ON—Linda Turner
Broken Arrow Ranch

Katherine Wyatt would never trust a man again, until she was forced to trust the sexy stranger at her family's ranch. Undercover investigator Hunter Sinclair wasn't looking to get romantically involved, especially with Katherine. But when she started dating a potential suspect, he had no choice but to let her in…and risk losing his heart.

#1509 THE DARK SIDE OF NIGHT—Cindy Dees
H.O.T. Watch

Fleeing for his life, secret agent Mitch Perovski is given permission to use the senator's boat as an out…but he didn't think he'd have the senator's daughter to accompany him. Kinsey Hollingsworth just wanted to escape the scandal she was mixed up in. Now she's thrown into a game of cat and mouse and her only chance for survival is Mitch. Can she withstand their burning attraction long enough to stay alive?

#1510 LETHAL ATTRACTION—Diana Duncan
Forever in a Day

When Sabrina Matthews is held at gunpoint, the last person she expects to save her life was SWAT pilot—and ex-crush—Grady O'Rourke. Grady is shocked when he receives a call informing him his next mission is to protect Sabrina. Though Grady is confident in his skills, she is the only woman who can get under his skin. He may be in greater danger of losing his heart than his life.

SRSCNM0308